HOW NANOTECHNOLOGY WILL IMPACT SOCIETY

by John Hakala

ReferencePoint Press®

San Diego, CA

TECHNOLOGY'S IMPACT

Printed in the United States

For more information, contact:
ReferencePoint Press, Inc.
PO Box 27779
San Diego, CA 92198
www.ReferencePointPress.com

LIBRARY OF CONGRESS CATALOGING-IN-PUBLICATION DATA

Name: Hakala, John, 1989– author.
Title: How Nanotechnology Will Impact Society / by John Hakala.
Description: San Diego, CA : ReferencePoint Press, Inc., [2019] | Series: Technology's Impact | Includes bibliographical references and index. | Audience: Grades 9 to 12.
Identifiers: LCCN 2018011545 (print) | LCCN 2018013171 (ebook) | ISBN 9781682824962 (ebook) | ISBN 9781682824955 (hardback)
Subjects: LCSH: Nanotechnology—Juvenile literature. | Nanostructured materials—Social aspects—Juvenile literature.
Classification: LCC T174.7.H34 2019 (ebook) | LCC T174.7.H34 2019 (print) | DDC 620/.5—dc23
LC record available at https://lccn.loc.gov/2018011545

Contents

IMPORTANT EVENTS IN THE DEVELOPMENT OF NANOTECHNOLOGY

1959
Richard Feynman gives a famous lecture called "There's Plenty of Room at the Bottom."

1974
Norio Taniguchi coins the term *nanotechnology*.

1985
The buckyball, a useful nanoparticle made from carbon atoms, is discovered.

1986
The atomic force microscope is invented, allowing scientists to manipulate matter on a tiny scale.

1989
Researchers create the IBM logo out of 35 individual atoms of xenon.

1991
Sumio Iijima discovers carbon nanotubes, amazingly versatile nanoparticles made up of carbon atoms.

1950 1960 1970 1980 1990 2000

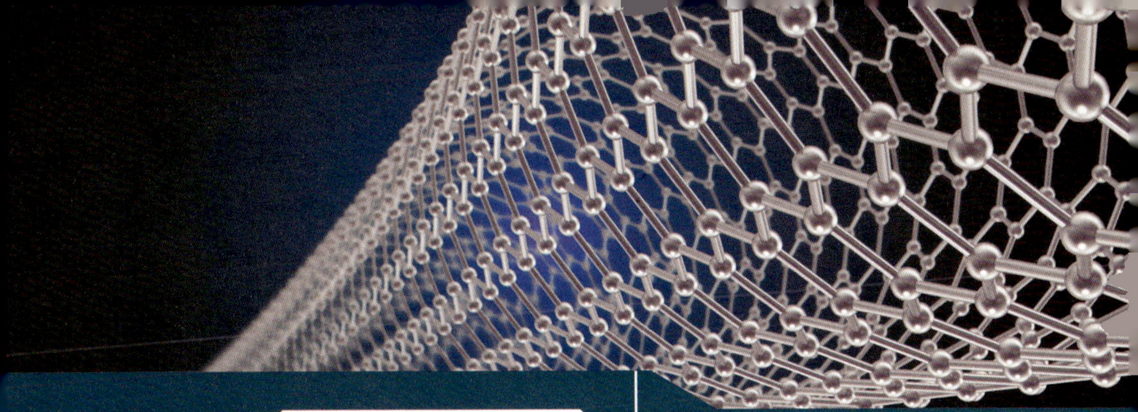

2000 2005 2010 2015 2020

2003
The US Congress passes the 21st Century Nanotechnology Research and Development Act.

2004
A nanomaterial called graphene is discovered.

2008
Controversial nanotechnology-based swimsuits are used in the Olympic Games.

2010
Nanoshells, which attack tumors while leaving surrounding tissue intact, are first used in humans for cancer treatment.

2012
The FlashBattery system, capable of extremely rapid charging, is developed.

2015
Carbon nanotubes are found in the lungs of children in Paris, France.

2016
Fabric constructed of carbon nanotubes that help protect against chemical agents is invented.

2017
A nanotechnology-based scaffold is used on injured animals to treat bone fractures.

Saved by Atoms

Time was running out for Hercules. The alpaca was only a few months old, and he was suffering badly. In 2017, during the animal's first day of life, he broke his leg on a ranch in Tennessee. It was a complicated and serious fracture, as it left the bone exposed. This led to the bone becoming infected. A bone infection can lead to a potentially deadly condition called osteomyelitis. This ailment involves the inflammation of bone marrow, an important tissue for maintaining overall health. Usually, the only treatment is bottle-feeding, routine injections, and hope.

That was the treatment plan before Hercules received a second opinion. At the University of Tennessee College of Veterinary Medicine (UTCVM), Dr. Pierre-Yves Mulon inspected the alpaca. Mulon suggested a revolutionary new device called the NuCress **scaffold**.

The NuCress scaffold was developed at the Center for Integrative Nanotechnology Sciences (CINS), part of the University of Arkansas Little Rock. The scaffold is a device used to regenerate bone material. It makes use of the cutting-edge science of nanotechnology. Nanotechnology is the practice of manipulating individual atoms and molecules to improve products, modify them, or create entirely new ones. The device is implanted into the fracture site and loaded with medications that promote healing. Tiny molecular machines in the device interact directly with bone tissue and stimulate bone-building cells called **osteoblasts**. Not only can this implant support a healing fracture and fight infections, but it can eliminate the need for additional treatment and surgery.

Nanotechnology is starting to play a role in medicine. Treatments like the one that was used on Hercules the alpaca will start making their way into human patients.

"He was able to walk immediately after surgery and has been very active," said Mulon.[1] Hercules is on the road to recovery back at the ranch. Dr. Mulon adds, "Any open fracture carries a guarded to poor prognosis, and Hercules made it, and we are very happy."[2] The makers of the NuCress scaffold plan to test the device in humans.

NANO IS NOW

Other medical applications of nanotechnology in use today include improved cancer treatments, more accurate disease diagnoses, and the prevention

WORDS IN CONTEXT

scaffold
A framework designed to support structures.

osteoblasts
A cell that produces chemicals that build bone tissue.

of deadly illnesses. But the medical industry is just one place where nanotechnology is being integrated into today's world.

Nanotechnology is also found in many everyday products. Deodorant, sunscreens, and waterproof clothing often include nanoparticles, objects ranging in size from 1 to 100 nanometers. Juan Hinestroza, the director of the Textiles Nanotechnology Laboratory at Cornell University, says, "We want to transform traditional natural fibers into true engineering materials that are multifunctional and that can be customized to any demand."[3]

The environment is also benefiting from achievements in nanotechnology. Nanoparticles are being used to clean pollution from air, water, and soil. "I believe nanotechnology will be seen as environmentally friendly and the critical element in environmental solutions," asserts Scott Rickert, CEO of nanotechnology company Nanofilm.[4] Advancing nanotechnology could also help in the fight against climate change.

THE MOLECULAR FUTURE

Nanotechnology operates in a tiny world invisible to the naked eye. On the smallest scale, all of the objects in the universe are made up of components called atoms. Different types of atoms have different numbers of particles called protons. The number of protons is what separates atoms of one element from atoms of another. For example, carbon, hydrogen, and oxygen are three common elements. Carbon has six protons in each atom, hydrogen has one proton in each atom, and oxygen has eight protons in each atom. The number of protons per atom is known as an element's atomic number. Atoms join together to form molecules. When 12 carbon atoms, 22 hydrogen atoms, and 11 oxygen atoms combine, they form a well-known molecule: sucrose, also known as sugar.

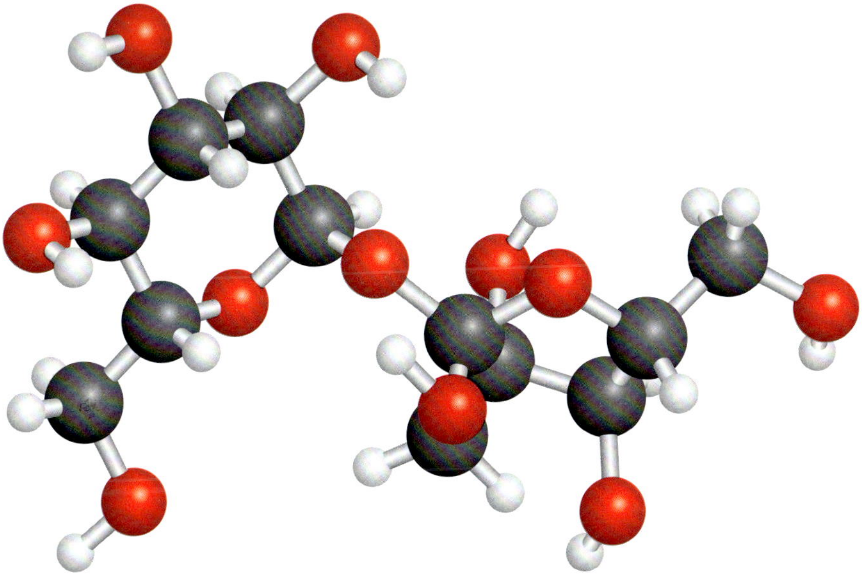

Atoms join together to form molecules, and these molecules make up living things and the world around us. Nanotechnology offers the chance to manipulate these tiny particles on an individual scale.

Nanotechnologists are able to manipulate individual atoms and molecules, making it possible to create incredible materials and structures with useful properties. The future of medicine, transportation, and the military may be defined by molecular manipulation. Surgical nanorobots, cheaper environmentally friendly fuels, and nanotechnology-enhanced battle armor may seem like science fiction now, but as technology advances they could become reality.

The time to bridge the gap between current science and future technology is now. However, scientists are proceeding with caution. Any new technology must be evaluated for risks. Research scientist and author Robert A. Freitas Jr. says, “We need to take seriously the prospects for molecular nanotechnology, personal nanofactories and nanorobotics, and attempt to understand the societal and political consequences of these technologies now, before it is too late.”[5] If nanotechnology can live up to the excitement, it will have the potential to improve society in many ways.

Chapter 1

How Does Nanotechnology Work?

The technological advances of today make this a time unlike any other. Science and technology are rapidly moving forward. It seems nearly every day there is a new innovation that aims to change and improve society. Many of the new products and ideas that make lives better are being driven by nanotechnology. The scientists working in the field of nanotechnology are unlocking the answers to previously unknown mysteries of the world. They are harnessing these secrets to dramatically change everyday items.

MODERN HISTORY AND SCIENTISTS BEHIND NANOTECHNOLOGY

In order to understand where nanotechnology is today, it is necessary to recognize how it came into existence. Like many major scientific developments, a lot of effort was required to make significant breakthroughs. What makes nanotechnology different from other projects in science and engineering is the decision to focus on the very small rather than the very large. The first public discussion of this shift came in a lecture in Pasadena, California.

Dr. Richard Feynman was a pioneer in the field of quantum mechanics. This field studies the behavior of the incredibly small. Focused on the motion and interactions of subatomic particles, the tiny components that make up atoms, quantum mechanics

Richard Feynman spoke about the promise of manipulating matter on a tiny scale. His work inspired future scientists as they developed modern nanotechnology.

began to shed light on the science that would lead to the age of nanotechnology. In 1950, after helping the US government develop the atomic bomb, Feynman became a professor of theoretical physics at the California Institute of Technology.

Many consider Dr. Feynman to be the father of modern nanotechnology. In 1959, Feynman gave a lecture titled "There's Plenty of Room at the Bottom." During this talk, he discussed the possibility of manipulating matter on the molecular level. Feynman explained that scientists might someday be able to "arrange the atoms the way we want."[6] This was a major shift in the way scientists thought about the future of technology. Scientists had a very limited view of the microscopic level. It was difficult to view individual atoms during this time. It was hard to believe humans could manipulate these fundamental building blocks one at a time.

In his lecture, Feynman speculated on the potential benefits of manipulating things on a tiny scale. He spoke about the impact on the future of computer science, stating, "When our computers get faster and faster and more and more elaborate, we will have to make them smaller and smaller."[7] Richard Feynman would go on to win the Nobel Prize in Physics in 1965 for his contributions to the field of physics.

ANSWERING FEYNMAN'S CHALLENGE

At the conclusion of Feynman's famous lecture, he proposed challenges to his audience. One of them was as follows: "It is my intention to offer a prize of $1,000 to the first guy who can take the information on the page of a book and put it on an area 1/25,000 smaller in linear scale in such manner that it can be read by an electron microscope." The challenge went unmet for nearly thirty years.

In 1985, Stanford University graduate student Thomas Newman attempted to solve the challenge with the help of his advisor R. Fabian Pease. Newman found a suitable book from Pease's bookshelf, the famous Charles Dickens novel *A Tale of Two Cities*. They etched the text of the first page onto a plastic square using an electron beam. Then they sent photos of the sample to Feynman. The pair wasn't sure if the photos would be good enough proof for him, as the image quality was rough.

Shortly after sending in the sample, the Stanford scientists received a congratulatory letter from Feynman—including a $1,000 check. Newman went on to focus his career on lithography, which is an important technique in the science of nanotechnology.

Richard P. Feynman, "There's Plenty of Room at the Bottom," *American Physical Society*, November 18, 2017. aps.org.

But it would take more time for his ideas about manipulating atoms and molecules to become reality.

In 1974, scientist Norio Taniguchi coined and defined the term *nanotechnology*. Taniguchi was a professor at the Tokyo University of Science. His work was focused on **semiconductor** technology, which operates at the nanometer level. Taniguchi described nanotechnology as a field that "consisted of the processing, separation, consolidation, and deformation of materials by one atom or one molecule."[8]

WORDS IN CONTEXT

semiconductor
A substance that can be manipulated to conduct or resist the flow of electricity in a useful way.

The 1980s saw the dawn of a new era of nanotechnology. This era would propel the field into the next century. The team of Sir Harold Kroto, Richard Smalley, and Robert Curl, working at Rice University in Texas, discovered incredibly important objects called fullerenes, spherical molecules formed from carbon atoms. This discovery would later go on to win the team the Nobel Prize in Chemistry in 1996. The work of Sumio Iijima brought attention to another notable object, the carbon nanotube (CNT), in 1991. A CNT is a molecule made up of carbon atoms. The atoms are arranged into a tubular shape. This structure gives them useful properties, including strength and electrical conductivity.

In 1986, Eric Drexler of the Massachusetts Institute of Technology (MIT) wrote a book titled *Engines of Creation: The Coming Era of Nanotechnology*. This text combined Feynman's ideas with Taniguchi's term in describing the idea of a microscopic machine that would be able to build copies of itself. Drexler explained that at such small sizes, machines might be able to work amazingly quickly. He compared such machines to the biological machinery at work inside plants and animals: "Nature shows that molecules can serve as machines because living things work by means of such machinery."[9] Drexler's book predicted many of the breakthroughs that were yet to come.

Intense interest in nanotechnology continued into the 2000s. In 2003, President George W. Bush signed the 21st Century Nanotechnology Research and Development Act. This piece of legislation made nanotechnology research a national priority. The act stated that its goal was "developing a fundamental understanding of matter that enables control and manipulation at the nanoscale."[10] The act further solidified the importance and promise that nanotechnology carried for the United States and the world. Feynman, Taniguchi, and other pioneering scientists laid the groundwork for the field of nanotechnology. They saw the field move from theories and speculation into reality in labs around the world.

WAS NANOTECHNOLOGY USED BEFORE ITS DISCOVERY?

Nanoscience wasn't knowingly discovered and explored until the twentieth century. However, there are several examples of nanomaterials being used in history. Their makers were unaware of the nanoparticles. These particles just happened to be an unseen product of the processes that craftsmen used. Nanomaterials showed up in tools of war and inspiring art. Only recently have we developed the technology to identify them.

Damascus steel, a metal used to make amazingly sharp swords, had CNTs in it. Historians believe this incidental use gave the warriors who used Damascus blades an advantage. These swords were used from the 1100s to the 1700s. The process for creating these weapons was a closely guarded secret. They were said to be able to

Damascus steel features complex patterns in its surface. Similar types of steel are still made today for use in knives and other tools.

cut a feather in half in midair while maintaining their sharpness over the course of several battles. The combination of superior sharpness and durability was unlike any weapon the world had ever seen. The nanotechnology-based sword may have altered the course of history.

It wasn't until 2006 that scientists discovered the steel blades contained traces of CNTs. The exact method in which these blades were made has been lost in history, but it is believed the legendarily sharp and durable blades were created from steel that originated in India. As Indian steel exports dropped, the superior blades became a relic of the past.

Another example of premodern nanotechnology is the famous European stained glass window. Artists from the medieval period experimented with various chemicals to create incredibly vibrant stained glass. They were unaware that they were tinkering with gold and silver nanoparticles. When gold chloride was added to melted glass, the end product was a red tint. Using silver nitrate resulted in a yellow finish. After analyzing the stained glass, modern scientists discovered the works were a result of nanoparticles, as gold and silver nanoparticles reflect red and yellow light, respectively.

The oldest known use of nanotechnology dates back nearly 1,600 years. The Romans created the Lycurgus Cup. The mysterious chalice contained a mixture of gold and silver nanoparticles. When illuminated from the front, the cup appeared red. When lit from behind, the cup was green. It wasn't until 1990 that British researchers were able to analyze broken fragments of the glass. University of Illinois-Champaign engineer Gang Logan Liu commented, "The Romans knew how to make and use nanoparticles for beautiful art."[11] The cup is now on display at the British Museum.

THE SCIENCE BEHIND THE TECHNOLOGY

Before studying how nanotechnology is at work in the world today, it is important to first understand just how small the world of nanotechnology truly is. A nanometer is one billionth of a meter. It is impossible to see such a small distance with the naked eye. In one inch, there are 25.4 million nanometers. A single sheet of newspaper is 100,000 nanometers thick. These are incredibly small distances compared to the visible world.

Nanotechnology typically involves objects that fall within the dimensions of 1 and 100 nanometers. At this miniscule level, matter looks and behaves differently than it does on a larger scale. Discovering the properties of nanoscale objects will help unlock their potential. Some of the properties that can be altered by scientists at the nano level include strength, magnetism, the ability to direct the flow of electricity, and how chemically reactive the material is. To be able to understand these properties, scientists must be able to observe them. To make this possible, they needed to invent a device capable of magnifying objects all the way down to the atomic level.

THE ATOMIC FORCE MICROSCOPE

Similar to a carpenter or an artist, the nanotechnologist must have the proper tools and techniques in order to carry out his or her work. There is one tool that is far more important than any other in this field. It gives scientists the capability to enter the world of the tiny. This portal to the atomic level is called the atomic force microscope (AFM). This development of the AFM made it possible for engineers to work with new types of resources called **nanomaterials**.

> **WORDS IN CONTEXT**
>
> **nanomaterial**
>
> A material that is measured on the nano scale, or one which is created by nanotechnology.

Before the AFM, the most powerful microscope was called the electron microscope. This device was not adequate to explore the nano world. In his 1959 speech, Feynman even challenged scientists by asking, "Is there no way to make the electron microscope more powerful?"[12] Answering this call, the AFM was developed in 1986 at IBM by Gerd Binnig, Calvin Quate, and Christoph Gerber. The AFM forever changed the way scientists could see, measure, and manipulate the world at a tiny scale. This type of microscope is so powerful that it is capable of distinguishing between fractions of nanometers.

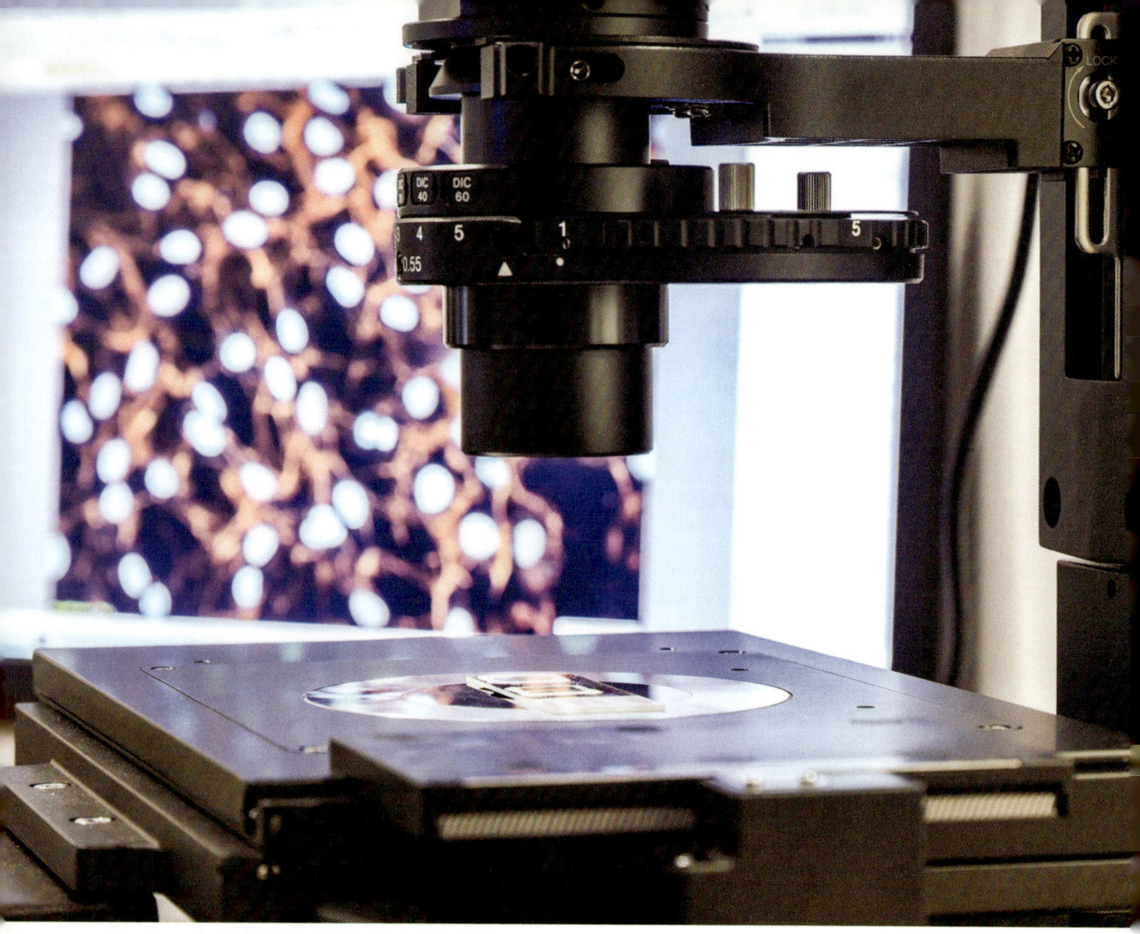

Atomic force microscopes are key to the work of nanotechnology researchers. These complex devices can cost tens of thousands of dollars or more.

Using incredibly sensitive electronics and an extremely sharp probe, a nanotechnologist can scan the surface of ultrafine materials. The AFM uses a laser beam to sense the forces given off by the molecules of the surface being scanned by the probe. Based upon the laser's feedback, the AFM creates a map of the surface. The nanotechnologist can then use the AFM to either observe or change the structure of the material under study. In 1989, IBM scientist Don Eigler demonstrated the amazing power of this microscope by creating a nano version of the company's three-letter logo. This was done by individually placing 35 atoms of the element xenon onto a nickel plate. It still remains the world's smallest corporate logo.

CARBON, GRAPHENE, AND FULLERENES

Carbon is likely the most important element in the world of nanomaterials. It is a highly versatile atom with the ability to create four separate bonds with other atoms. In nature, carbon is critical to living things and nonliving objects alike. An entire branch of chemistry, organic chemistry, is dedicated to carbon compounds. Carbon can create extremely strong bonds with other carbon atoms, making useful molecules for nanotechnologists. These carbon-based arrangements can take several forms.

Carbon's forms vary significantly in their physical properties. Both graphite and diamonds are created from this element. The same element that creates the writing material of a pencil also makes up diamonds that can cost many thousands of dollars. Graphite is a relatively soft material, while diamonds are among the hardest. The difference isn't in the ingredients, but in the way the molecules are arranged. Diamonds are made up of a three-dimensional array of strongly bonded carbon atoms. Graphite consists of stacks of weakly bonded carbon sheets. The arrangement of the materials' structure makes all the difference.

The strongest man-made material is also made out of carbon. Graphene is a single transparent sheet of carbon atoms arranged hexagonally. It is considered to be one of the most critical discoveries in nanotechnology. The basic structure is just one atom thick, making it the thinnest material on Earth. Graphene conducts electricity extremely well, making it very useful in electronics. Graphene is also used in medical, industrial, and chemical technologies. Due to its flexibility, strength, and light weight, it can be used in a variety of different ways.

Fullerenes are molecules of carbon that are manipulated into particular shapes, including tubes and spheres. Thanks to carbon's strong bonds, these structures have impressive mechanical strength. This is the ability to hold up against the stress of physical forces. To go along with their physical toughness, fullerenes can also conduct electricity well. This property is important in the design and creation of nano-based electronic components.

The most well-known fullerenes are CNTs and Buckminsterfullerene. The latter, which is a group of 60 carbon atoms arranged into a spherical shape, is named in honor of American designer, author, and inventor Richard Buckminster Fuller. Some refer to these structures as buckyballs, given their round shape.

THE AMAZING CARBON NANOTUBE

CNTs are important structures with astonishing properties. Although they are 10,000 times thinner than a human hair, by weight they are stronger than steel. CNTs are made from material similar to graphite found in a pencil, but the difficulty in making them means that they are extremely expensive. Despite high costs, their usage has been increasing in recent years. Nanotechnology researcher Michael De Volder explained in 2014, "Since 2006, worldwide carbon nanotube production capacity has increased at least tenfold."

CNTs have the capability to reach into all aspects of life. They can be used to clean water, generate electricity from sunlight, create bulletproof vests, and serve as the building blocks of touch screens in phones or tablets. They may also play a significant role in designing revolutionary computers that will enhance artificial intelligence. The possibilities are only limited by the imagination of nanotechnology researchers.

Quoted in "Carbon Nanotubes Find Real World Applications," *University of Cambridge*, March 31, 2014. eng.cam.ac.uk.

NANOPARTICLES

To be considered a nanoparticle, a structure must be less than 100 nanometers in one or more dimension. These supersmall particles may act much differently than a bulk material made out of the same type of atoms. For example, copper nanoparticles are physically very hard and strong. However, a copper pipe is relatively flexible and soft. One of the most important tasks for nanotechnologists is discovering and understanding how nanoparticles behave differently than the same materials at larger sizes.

Nanoparticles for use in chemistry are often employed as **catalysts**. One area where nanoparticle catalysts may be used is in vehicles. Cars that run on gasoline include components called catalytic converters. A catalytic converter takes the emissions produced by the engine and removes some of their more toxic components using chemical reactions. This process makes vehicle emissions less harmful to the environment. By improving the efficiency of the chemical reactions in catalytic converters, nano catalysts may be helpful in decreasing air pollution.

> **WORDS IN CONTEXT**
>
> **catalyst**
> A substance that speeds up a chemical reaction.

MANIPULATING ATOMS AND NANOMATERIAL

There are several ways in which scientists can manipulate objects on the nano scale. One of the techniques is called dip pen nanolithography (DPN). This technique involves dipping the AFM's probe into a chemical fluid. The fluid on the tip of the probe is then used to write on a surface atom by atom. This process is similar to writing with a pen and paper. In 1996, IBM used DPN to create the world's smallest abacus. This type of primitive calculating device, which uses beads that slide across rows of wire, was once used for simple math. Scientists working for IBM in Switzerland developed the nanoabacus by creating multiple rows of ten molecules placed on a copper surface. These "beads" were individual molecules of buckminsterfullerene that were put in place by the DPN method. The scientists were able to push the buckyball beads with the tip of the AFM probe in the same way a person slides the beads along the wire of an abacus.

DNA NANOMACHINES

Another method for creating nanomaterials is by realizing Drexler's idea of self-assembling nanomachines. This model of creating nanomaterials is considered the bottom-up approach. In theory, it could make the manufacturing of nanomaterials easier than ever before. But self-assembly isn't as easy as throwing the ingredients together and hoping for the best. Researchers are searching for ways to make nanomachines that build themselves.

One key inspiration comes from a chemical in nature that is capable of copying and assembling itself: deoxyribonucleic acid (DNA). DNA is found in every living cell. It contains the genetic instructions that tell the body how to make every part of the organism. Part of its job is to copy itself so that cells can reproduce and each maintain a complete set of DNA. DNA is made up of a long series of base pairs, sets of specific chemicals that pair with each other. These pairings represent the coded genetic information.

Since the 1980s, New York University chemist Ned Seeman has been studying how to use the natural pairing and assembling process to create nano-scale structures. One of his inventions is a group of DNA strands that join together like interlocking tiles. Another is DNA

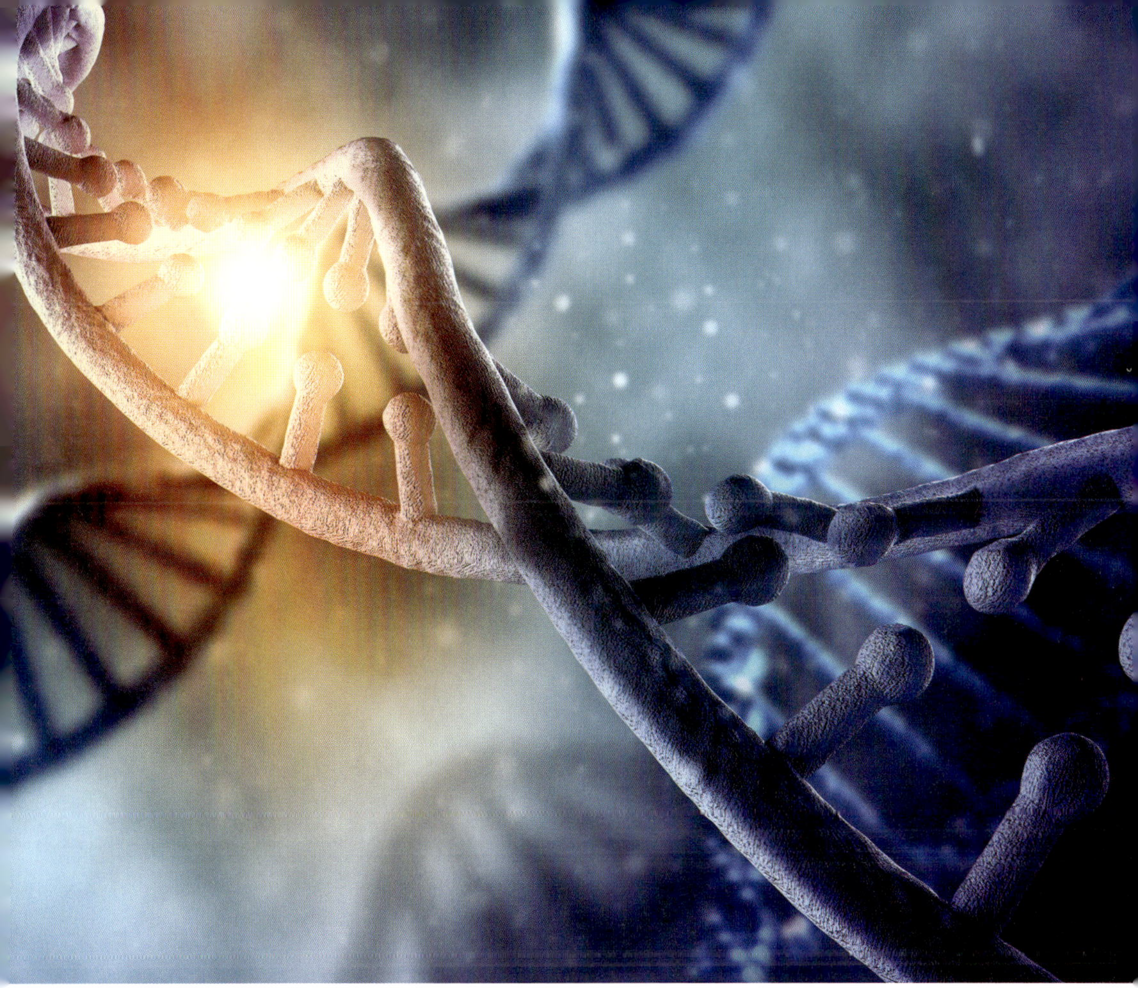

DNA is capable of copying itself and assembling molecules into specific shapes. Researchers hope to harness these properties to create nanoscale machines.

that forms itself into a three-dimensional shape. He has even created nanomachines that move by sliding along DNA strands. He says, "DNA is the world's greatest architectural material, in my opinion."[13]

Other scientists have built upon Seeman's pioneering work. Duke University's Thom LaBean has studied how to use DNA's assembly properties to make tiny machines that respond to signals in the body. For instance, if the body is under attack by cancer or a virus, it gives off certain chemical messages. A nanomachine could recognize these messages and release other chemicals to fight off the attack.

SCIENCE BECOMING TECHNOLOGY

Once researchers learned how to manipulate atoms and molecules, the next challenge was to take this ability and use it for practical purposes. This is where the science of research is translated into real-world technology, a process that happens in any field of study. Describing this transition, theoretical physicist Edward Teller said, "The science of today is the technology of tomorrow."[14]

> **WORDS IN CONTEXT**
>
> **ultraviolet radiation**
> A type of energy emitted by the sun that can damage materials and living tissue.

When it is possible to alter the basic composition of materials, there is an opportunity to greatly improve them. Nanotechnologists can enhance products to make them stronger, lighter, more durable, better able to repel fluids, more resistant to **ultraviolet radiation**, better able to fight bacteria, more resistant to scratches, or better able to conduct electricity. Further research will allow nanotechnologists to tap into the potential of these newly discovered molecular properties. Nanotechnology will certainly bring changes to everyday life. In many cases it already has.

Although the world of nanotechnology exists on the scale of atoms and molecules, the consequences of its use are quite enormous. Researchers all over the world are harnessing this science to shape the future of civilization. The health-care industry, the environment, and even everyday products will be impacted by significant advances in nanotechnology. There have been many debates over whether this will be a good or bad concept to pursue. Before a discussion of the future benefits and risks, there must first be an evaluation of how and where nanotechnology is being applied today.

THE NANO SCALE

OBJECT	SIZE	
Ant	5 million nanometers	
Human hair	60,000 nanometers	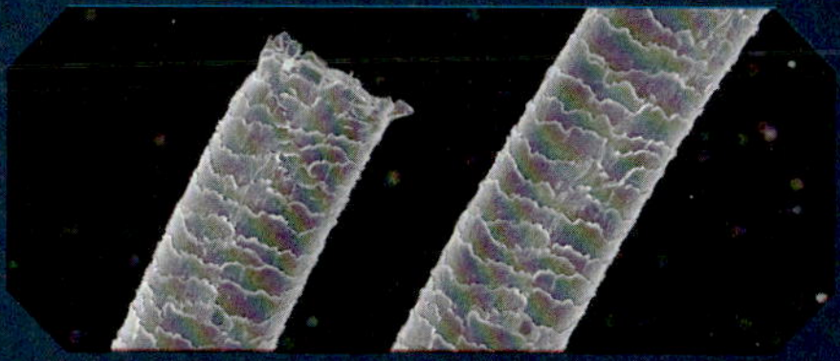
Red blood cell	7,000 nanometers	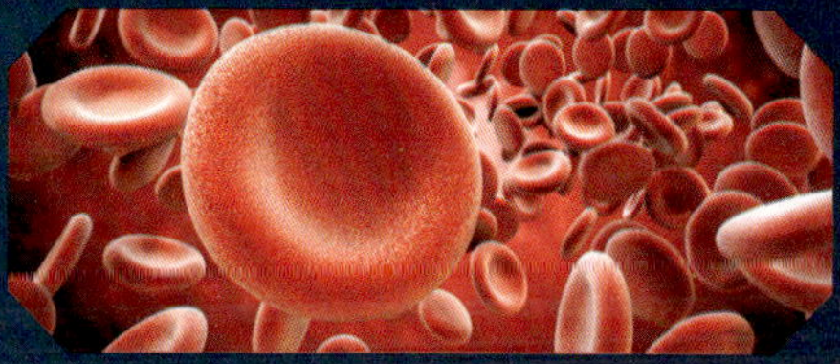
DNA	2.5 nanometers	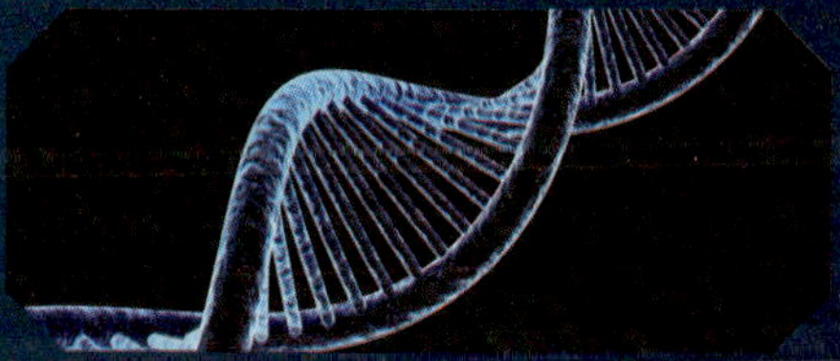
Carbon nanotube	1.3 nanometers	
Carbon atom	0.2 nanometers	

Chapter 2

Where Is Nanotechnology Found Today?

The world is a constantly changing place. The revolution of nanotechnology has sped up the pace of advancements in technology, and it will continue to do so. While a lot of the technology of tomorrow is currently in the research and development phases, the world has already seen amazing products that contain nanomaterials. Some technology is widely recognized and familiar. Other ideas and items make unexpected use of nanotechnology. A few of the fields in which it has had the greatest impact include medicine, consumer products, the environment, and the world of sports. Some ideas have been greatly welcomed and appreciated, while others have been highly controversial.

NANOTECHNOLOGY TAKES ON CANCER

Some of the deadliest diseases in the world today are cancers. Many people have known someone who has been affected by these diseases. Cancer can appear in several forms, and it is capable of affecting nearly every organ system. Each type of cancer is different. This trait makes cancers difficult to fully understand and treat. Scientists have been exhaustively researching treatment options and cures for several decades. Nanotechnology now joins the fight in the diagnosis and treatment of this vicious ailment.

In general, cancer involves excessive cell growth, creating what are known as tumors. The cancer can spread, leading to multiple tumors throughout the body. A method has been designed to use cancer's own hallmark characteristics against it. When a tumor forms within the body it needs to create its own blood supply. This process is called angiogenesis. When new blood vessels are used by cancerous cells, the pathways are different from normal blood vessels. There are gaps in the vessel tissue which can be anywhere from hundreds of nanometers to a few **microns** in size. This is where nanoparticles can help save the patient. Nanoparticles have been developed to block these gaps. This process creates a direct pathway for drugs called **chemotherapeutics** to attack the tumors. Without these nanoparticles, these drugs could potentially leak out into healthy tissue. This would create unintended damage or further illness.

WORDS IN CONTEXT

micron
One millionth of a meter.

chemotherapeutics
Drugs designed to kill spreading cancer.

There is a new method that utilizes nanoparticles to fight cancers of the head and neck. A drug known as AuroShell is a gold nanoshell that targets the site of a tumor. Nanoshells are microscopic spherical structures with a silica core that can be loaded with a variety of useful chemicals. Once the nanoshells find their way into the tumor, an infrared light is applied externally to the body over the site of the cancer. This process gradually heats the nanoparticles, which destroys the tumor while doing minimal damage to healthy cells nearby. This is especially important due to the presence of many sensitive structures in the head and neck. The use of drugs like

AuroShell may go on to save lives and greatly improve the quality of life patients experience after beating the disease.

Another cancer fighting system is currently in the development phase. It uses magnetic properties of nanoparticles to accurately deliver drugs. University of Georgia graduate student Andrey Zakharchenko says, "We showed that we can deliver anti-cancer drugs exactly in the area where they are needed and they can kill cancer cells."[15] Two different kinds of nanoparticles would be used. One type would carry the chemotherapeutics. The other would hold enzymes.

Once a magnetic field is applied over the patient, the two nanoparticles would merge, creating a forced reaction that delivers the medication in a specified location. The location is determined by controlling when and where the magnet is applied. Besides the precise targeting, researchers also believe a major benefit of this technique will be the prevention of common chemotherapeutic side effects, such as heart damage or hair loss.

DETECTION

Another critically important tool in the world of cancer treatment is the use of **diagnostic** imaging. Nanoparticles are currently being used to enhance imaging to better diagnose diseases. Lee Josephson of Harvard Medical School has shown how magnetic iron-based nanoparticles with fluorescent tags can be used to enhance pictures obtained from magnetic resonance imaging (MRI). MRI technology uses magnets and radio waves to generate images of the inside of a patient's body.

WORDS IN CONTEXT

diagnostic
Dealing with the detection of diseases or injuries.

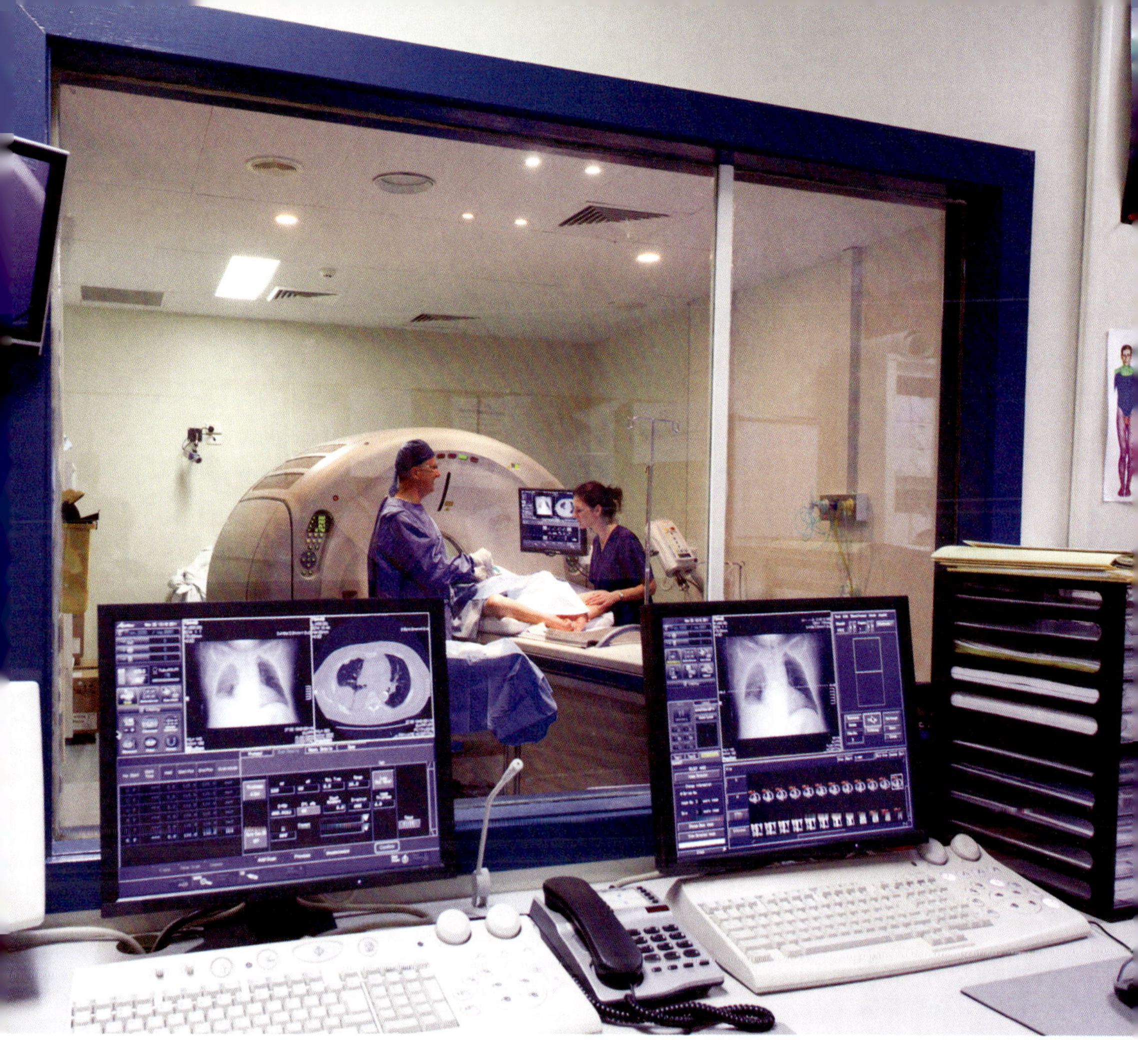

MRI machines make it possible to see inside a patient's body. Nanotechnology can help make it even easier to see specific things in the body.

In Josephson's method, the nanoparticles can selectively seek out either normal or cancerous cells. The nanoparticles then help these areas show up clearly on an MRI scan. They act as contrast agents, substances that make structures inside the body easier to see when viewed with a medical scanning technology. This gives doctors a better idea as to where the disease is located or how far it has spread. Furthermore, Josephson explains, "If you inject [the particles] 6 or even 12 hours prior to an operation, you will be able to see where they are intraoperatively."[16] In other words, the fluorescent tags will

BULLETPROOF SHIRTS

Imagine the possibility of wearing a shirt that is pound-for-pound stronger than steel yet weighs as little as a feather. That day may be coming soon. Thanks to CNTs, researchers have developed nanomaterials that may soon replace standard bulletproof materials. "We want to create new-generation fibers that exhibit both superior strength and toughness," states Horacio Espinosa, a professor of mechanical engineering at Northwestern University. These nanomaterials have shown incredible strength and versatility. They have not shown up in clothing yet, but early studies of these materials have been promising.

Tests have been done in which a glass bullet shot the nanomaterial at three times the speed of a standard military rifle. The results were incredible. The sheets of CNTs absorbed the projectile. A person would have been safe standing behind it. This may be an amazing breakthrough for military and law enforcement organizations. The materials are far lighter and more flexible than Kevlar, the standard synthetic fiber currently used for bulletproof vests. This will not only better protect people wearing this protective gear, but it will make their jobs easier by making the gear lighter and better-fitting.

Quoted in Grant Banks, "Engineers Create New Nano-fiber Tougher than Kevlar," *New Atlas*, December 7, 2010. newatlas.com.

make the particles visible to a surgeon as he or she operates. This type of technology may make the cancer easier to find and remove during surgery.

Scientists have also unleashed nanoparticles that are capable of carrying out more than one task. A report from the National Academy of Medicine notes, "Nanoparticles can also have multiple functions. Some combine drugs with contrast agents, while others might someday be engineered to treat, monitor the effectiveness of treatment, and then re-treat if the treatment is not working."[17] The report explains that the role of these nanoparticles is to "get the right treatments to the right patients at the right time."[18] Successfully fighting cancer is often based upon the timeliness of treatment.

As the war against cancer continues, nanotechnology is unleashing new ways to help tip the scales in favor of victory and health. Health-care professionals have implemented better methods of delivering medicine, destroying tumors, and locating diseases. While such concepts are exciting and important, they represent only the tip of the iceberg for nanotechnology's potential medical applications.

EVERYDAY NANOTECHNOLOGY

Clothing and hygienic products are critical to daily life. Sporting and recreational items improve the lives of people around the world. Nanotechnology has found its way into all these product categories, improving both the products' performance and the consumer's satisfaction.

After being exposed to sweat, many items of clothing, including gym shirts and socks, can smell awful. Fortunately, nanotechnology is capable of fighting these odors. Silver is being used in nanoparticle form. Nanosilver particles carry and release electrically charged **ions** into bacterial cells, which kills them. Bacteria are the main cause of these odors. Therefore, eliminating them will greatly decrease the smell. The clothing stays soft and wearable thanks to the small particle size, which does not alter the consistency of the fabric.

WORDS IN CONTEXT

ions
Atoms or molecules that have a positive or negative charge after gaining or losing electrons.

Nanotechnologists are helping people who love the outdoors through the use of the chemical silica. Nanoparticles of silica can be added into fabric or applied on its surface. This forms a coating that repels liquids. Silica-coated surfaces cause liquids to bead up and roll off. Nanotechnology can be used as the first line of defense against soaking and staining on things such as hiking boots, backpacks, and other camping gear. This could actually be a life-saving development. Waterproof camping and hiking equipment could lead to a decrease in the number of cases of hypothermia, as soaked clothes can lead to a decrease in body temperature.

A sunburn on the skin is the undesirable effect of prolonged sun exposure. "There is no degree of tanning, whether from natural sunlight or artificial light, like tanning beds, that can be considered safe," says clinical professor of dermatology Francesca Fusco.[19] A sunburn can simply be painful at the time, but in the long run it can have serious health effects. It can lead to the formation of skin cancers. Manufacturers have come up with a way to use sun-blocking technology and weave it into the fabric of clothing. Sun-blocking clothing uses titanium dioxide or zinc oxide nanoparticles. These nanoparticles are extremely effective at reflecting and scattering the ultraviolet (UV) rays of the sun, which are primarily responsible for sunburns and skin cancer.

COSMETIC APPLICATIONS

Every day, people use many types of products and materials to help them look and feel better. Nano-versions of substances called **emulsions** are being used in several familiar cosmetic products, including lotions and conditioners. Nanoparticles are also being used to help the body and mouth resist foul odors. Nanosilver is being

WORDS IN CONTEXT

emulsions
Small droplets of a substance that will not dissolve when suspended in another liquid.

utilized in deodorant, while nanogold is now found in toothpaste. Similar to odor-neutralizing clothing, both use bacteria-killing ions as disinfectants.

Nanoparticles are being used in sunscreen lotions, too. One reason people choose not to use sunscreen is because of the messy or uncomfortable residue left behind after application. Just as in sun-proof clothing, miniaturized titanium dioxide and zinc oxide particles are used in lotions to increase transparency and the ability to filter sunlight. Nanoparticle sunscreen lotions are more effective at blocking the harmful UV sun rays, and they don't leave behind a greasy, visible mess on skin after application. This might encourage people to use sunscreen more often. More consistent use of these products may help decrease future rates of skin cancer.

NANOTECHNOLOGY IN SPORTS

Nanomaterials are changing how games are played. Athletes are using this technology to push the limits of their athletic ability. Making equipment lighter, stronger, and faster can help when players are competing at the highest level. Nanotechnology can help improve all of these factors. Nanomaterials that are being used in sporting equipment today are already making a big difference.

In tennis, no piece of equipment is more important than the racquet. The sporting goods manufacturing company Wilson used nanotechnology to develop rackets that are 22 percent more powerful than previous models. CNTs are added to the frame of the tennis rackets, making them both lighter and stronger. Due to the decrease in weight, players will be able to swing the racket faster and more precisely. This allows for greater ball speed and control. In a game that can be decided by mere inches, that increase in performance can make all the difference.

An advanced swimsuit introduced in 2008 used nanoparticles in its design. Before long, a large number of top swimmers were using it.

Waterproof clothing can help keep the rain away. It can also help swimmers make Olympic history. In the 2008 Summer Olympic Games, swimmers used swimsuits designed with a silica-based nanoparticle coating. This technological change decreased water absorption by twenty-five times compared to previous materials. This was a controversial issue. Swimmers were easily shattering previous world records. Many believe this was due to the suits, not the athletes. In response to the controversy, the world governing body for competitive swimming banned the suits in competition starting on January 1, 2010. Critics argued that even this ban came too late. Sports journalist Christine Brennan said, "It was crystal clear that the world record pace was turning swimming into a joke. Anyone in the sport that had their eyes open could tell something was wrong."[20]

The swimsuit ban demonstrates just how powerful nanotechnology can be in sports. This incident has led to many debates about the use of nanotechnology and other advances in sporting equipment. Some believe that the technology will overshadow the performance of athletes or give unfair advantages to people who can afford the latest materials over others who can't.

Nanotechnology has other, less controversial roles in sports. In some uses, it can help to motivate and inspire a team. Working for New Zealand's national rugby team, Adidas created a jersey that used fiber-imprinting nanotechnology to etch the names of thousands of fans, and the names of all the team's players, into the fabric of the players' jerseys. The process was similar to that used to etch grooves onto **silicon** chips. The printing device allowed for more than 100 names to be written in a single millimeter. Team captain Richie McCaw stated, "Having the names of fans stitched onto the jerseys provides the players with a further reminder of the public support for the team."[21] The rugby team was inspired by literally carrying the fans on their backs.

WORDS IN CONTEXT

silicon
A chemical element often used in the production of electronics.

THE ART OF NANOTECHNOLOGY

Nanotechnology is showing up in places other than on store shelves and in life-saving technology. History has shown that art and science have a strong bond. Nanomaterials are quickly becoming subjects of works of art hung up on museum walls.

The Academy of NanoArt was founded by artist and scientist Cris Orfescu. He believes that, "NanoArt could be for the 21st Century what photography was for the 20th Century."[22] Images that were once never before visible by the public are now being transformed into artistic examples of natural and synthetic materials. Thanks to the AFM and other powerful microscopes, art exhibits are popping up around the world showing off the mysteries of the nanolandscape.

A common enhancement technique done by these scientist-artists is to digitally add color after the images are acquired. The microscope captures the images in black and white, leaving the artists with unique possibilities. Once the images are digitally altered, they are printed onto canvas or fine art paper for display.

Some of the artists create unique structures called nanosculptures strictly for artistic purposes. Perhaps the most famous example of nanosculpting in the United States is the work called "Nanobama." University of Michigan engineering professor John Hart created strikingly realistic images of President Barack Obama. Each face, only about 500 microns across, was comprised of 150 million CNTs.

The images may serve as inspiration for some to enter the field of nanotechnology. Others simply might enjoy the beauty of art on the atomic level. While NanoArt may not be an accessible medium for everyone to create, the images and sculptures are certainly

Human industrial activity releases huge amounts of pollution into the air. Proposed nanotechnology applications may offer a way to clean up some of that pollution.

worth appreciating. From the nanolandscape to the visible natural landscape, nanotechnology is creating exciting benefits.

NANOTECHNOLOGY CLEARS THE AIR

Nanotechnology has brought about new ways of protecting the environment. This includes the air we breathe, the water we drink, and the soil we use to grow food. While nanoparticles are tiny compared to the massive scope of the environment around us, they can still play a significant role in creating a cleaner world. Nanoparticles help clean existing contamination while assisting in the prevention of further damage.

Air pollution and contamination is an ongoing and serious problem. As developing countries begin to increase their industrial capabilities, more harmful gases are being released into the atmosphere. This could lead to a large increase in pollution and adverse health effects. In 2014, the World Health Organization stated, "around 7 million people died—one in eight of total global deaths—as a result of air pollution exposure."[23] This is an issue that requires immediate attention. Without a serious response, those numbers may very well go up. Fortunately, nanotechnology holds potential for addressing this problem.

The primary way nanostructures are able to help eliminate air pollution is through the process of adsorption. Adsorption occurs when layers of molecules stick to the surface of a solid or liquid. Carbon nanostructures are efficient at chemically binding to other substances, making them highly capable nanoadsorbents.

In particular, nanoadsorbents interact very well with organic contaminants such as the greenhouse gas carbon dioxide. Greenhouse gases are released into the atmosphere when people burn fossil fuels, such as oil and coal. These gases trap heat in the atmosphere, warming the planet over time in a process known as climate change. Using nanoadsorbents may be a critical breakthrough for the elimination of such harmful industrial-produced gases in the atmosphere. They may also be useful in removing other pollutants from the atmosphere, improving air quality.

IMPROVING OUR WATERS

Water is a critical resource for everyone on Earth. It is used for drinking, bathing, cleaning, and a wide array of industrial applications. Yet pollution can leave water undrinkable and unusable. Nanotechnology can help. Social innovation researcher Rosa Wang states, "Nanotechnology could offer solutions, not temporary fixes, to some of the most serious problems faced by humanity including water."[24] Much like air contaminant control, nanotechnology can use the process of adsorption to clean pollutants from water.

Having metal contaminants in water can create serious long-term health problems. Human bodies are not designed to efficiently eliminate these materials. Toxic levels of chemicals such as arsenic may cause both short and long-term effects in the form of poisoning and cancer. Filters that use nanotechnology, including CNTs, have been shown to be effective at eliminating metals from water.

NANOFARMING

Laboratory-created nanoparticles are helping increase the quality and quantity of the foods that farmers can grow. One example of nanotechnology being used today is nanofertilizer. Fertilizers help facilitate plant growth. These chemicals are incredibly important to farmers and to the world's food production. Nanofertilizer particles are small enough to be directly absorbed into the plant through the leaves. Leaf-absorption is beneficial because the nutrients are more efficiently taken up by this method. The nanoparticles won't need to be introduced into the soil. This breakthrough will increase **crop yields**, eliminate waste, and provide consumers with more food. "The only way to meet the demand is to significantly increase global food production," says German agricultural economist Clemens Breisinger.[25] Nanotechnology is one way that these productivity gains could be achieved.

WORDS IN CONTEXT

crop yields
The amount of harvested crops per unit of land.

Another valuable tool in the world of farming is the biosensor. Nanobiosensors are used to detect the nutrients and toxic substances in the soil. One potentially deadly bacterium called *E. coli* can be detected in soil using a nanofilm device made from the element bismuth. *E. coli* affects a person's digestive system after consuming contaminated meat or produce, causing food poisoning. When the bacteria are present, an electrical signal is passed through the detector. The farmer can then deal with the contamination problem directly and not send the affected products to market. Typically, an *E. coli* outbreak is not known until the contaminated product has

POWERED BY NANOTECHNOLOGY

Another way nanotechnology can help the environment is by making renewable energy sources more efficient. Renewable energy sources are those that are naturally replenished. In contrast, nonrenewable sources, such as coal and oil, are eventually used up. A limited amount of them is available on Earth. Renewable sources, such as solar panels and wind turbines, need only sunlight and the motion of wind to generate power.

As wind strikes the blades of a wind turbine, they begin to turn. When the blades turn, a generator inside the hub converts this motion into electricity. This electricity can be harvested for human use. A single large wind turbine can generate enough electricity to power hundreds of homes. Windmills are often found in groups on what are known as wind farms. This technology is especially advantageous in rural farming regions because the wind is blocked less by forests and structures. Wind farms can power entire towns.

Nanotechnology is being used to make wind turbines more efficient at generating electricity. Turbine blades can be created using a nanotube-based epoxy. This technology makes the blades significantly lighter. Having lighter blades means less wind is required to push them. This can boost electricity generation by 30 percent.

made many people sick. Getting ahead of the problem is a better strategy for ensuring food safety.

Nanotechnology may also find its way into chemicals such as yield-enhancing herbicides, substances that destroy weeds and other plants that compete with the desired crop. The current chemical-based versions of these treatments are controversial due to studies showing that they can harm the environment. New types of herbicides that use nanotechnology have been shown to cause minimal environmental damage while being effective at killing weeds. Nanoherbicides attack weeds by targeting and destroying weed seeds before they get a chance to grow.

Air, water, and soil are all critically important components of the environment. If one of these elements is negatively impacted, the damage could spread to the other two. Advances in nanotechnology will help protect all three.

Like any emerging technology, there is still a lot that needs to be understood about nanotechnology. Nanotechnology has proven itself in numerous applications today, but researchers expect it will find even more uses in the future. There are legitimate concerns that need to be addressed as the world begins to rely more upon nanotechnology. There must be an evaluation of potential risks, downfalls, and setbacks. While nanotechnology has great promise, if these issues are overlooked it could also bring significant problems.

Chapter 3

What Are the Risks of Nanotechnology?

When groundbreaking science becomes technology, there are many unknowns that must first be answered. New developments can bring great benefits, but there is also the potential for new risks and dangers. These issues must be addressed before a new technology enters widespread use. Nanotechnology researchers are working to predict and solve as many of these problems as possible before they arise. Scientist and author David Brin says, "A challenging, possibly daunting future rushes toward us. We need caution and skeptical worry. We also need ambition and problem-solving confidence."[26]

People's health, the environment, and public safety could potentially be endangered if nanotechnology is not used safely and appropriately. Some of the perceived risks of nanotechnology come from exaggerated science-fiction examples of the technology in action, but other threats are realistic. These factors could derail many of the positive impacts if the public cannot be convinced that the good outweighs the bad.

The excitement of possible breakthroughs may lead to the threat of risks being overlooked. The purpose of studying such risks is not to cause fear. If researchers understand how the technology can go wrong, they will have a chance to make it right before it is too late.

NANOTECHNOLOGY HEALTH RISKS

Nanotechnology advocate Bernie Marcus says, "Nanotechnology in medicine is going to have a major impact on the survival of the human race."[27] It has been shown that nanoparticles can be used to target specific problems within the body, such as cancer. There is plenty of potential for good in these drugs, but there is also a lot that is still unknown. Beyond medical uses of nanoparticles there may be unintended inhalation or **ingestion** of these materials. How will these tiny engineered particles interact with the complex systems inside the human body? Unfortunately, not much is known yet. The early indications of the potential risks do not look good.

WORDS IN CONTEXT

ingestion
The consumption of a substance by an organism.

dysrhythmia
An electrical malfunction of the heart.

Nanoparticles can unintentionally find their way into the air we breathe, creating a new type of pollution. Once the particles enter the body, they will find their way into the lungs. The tiny size of nanoparticles allows them to cross into the bloodstream and travel throughout the body by a process called translocation. A study from the University of Edinburgh proved that nanoparticles remain in the lungs for up to six hours after inhalation. These particles have also shown a tendency to travel to the heart, which can lead to serious cardiovascular problems.

A 2005 study reports that an increase in exposure to particles will lead to an increase in mortality due to **dysrhythmias**, heart failure, and cardiac arrest. Each of those conditions can be caused by an elevated heart rate, which in turn can be caused by exposure to carbon-based and titanium-oxide nanoparticles. These nanoparticles

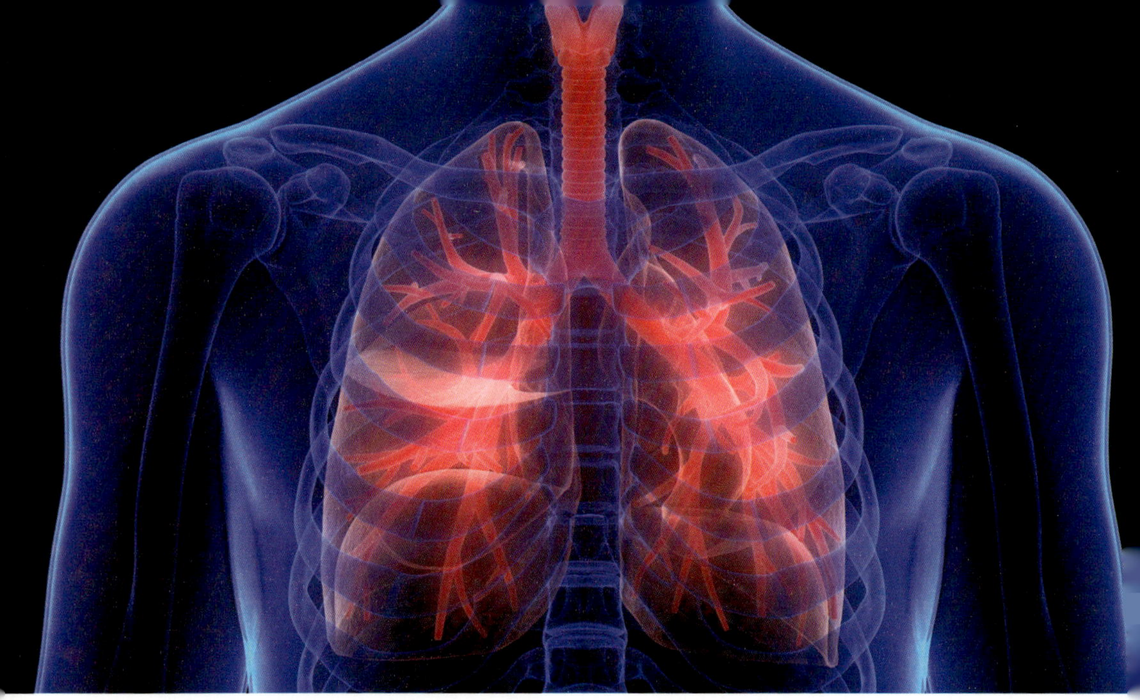

The lungs are sensitive organs, and their proper functioning is critical to people's health. The effects of nanoparticles on the lungs are still being studied, but experts believe they could be seriously harmful.

help trigger the release of noradrenaline, a hormone which increases heart rate. Dysrhythmias are problems with the electrical signals sent through the heart. Heart failure is when the heart muscle becomes less functional and has trouble getting blood to the lungs or the rest of the body. Cardiac arrest is when the heart completely stops beating and fails to provide blood to the rest of the body. All of these conditions can be deadly, and exposure to certain types of nanoparticles could contribute to them.

Before the particles move on from the lungs, they may create damage locally, which can cause serious problems. According to a report from Oxford University researchers, "Lung damage is the chief human toxicity concern surrounding nanotechnology."[28] Nanoparticles can create inflammation when deposited into lung tissue. Inflammation can be a dangerous and destructive process in the human body. In the lungs it can worsen asthma and chronic obstructive pulmonary disorder (COPD). Researchers suspect that lung cancer is also a possible danger, but long-term studies have not yet been conducted to prove this.

Another potentially dangerous scenario is the translocation of nanoparticles into the delicate nervous system. The nose is a highly effective sensory organ, and it has components directly connected to the brain. When nanoparticles are inhaled through the nose, they are taken up by a nasal structure called the olfactory bulb. The olfactory bulb is a round mass of tissue which receives information about smells and transmits this information to the brain through the olfactory nerve. If nanoparticles enter the nose they can take this same pathway directly into the brain. Whether they cause injury or toxicity in humans is still unknown.

In studies done on rats, nanoparticles of copper were introduced to the brain. The particles were shown to cause an inflammatory process that can be toxic to the nerve cells that make up brain tissue. The smaller the nanoparticle was, the worse the toxic effect it demonstrated was. Nanoparticles have demonstrated the ability to slip through cell **membranes**, which normally protect living tissue from foreign material. In a separate study, nanoparticles were shown to affect the brain's important defense system, the blood-brain barrier. This barrier is a selective membrane that allows helpful materials in and keeps harmful substances out. Serious problems can occur if nanoparticles create unintended pathways by punching holes through this barrier. One such issue is swelling of the brain. This condition, called cerebral edema, can be deadly.

WORDS IN CONTEXT

membrane

A barrier that allows some things through while stopping others.

With so many developments occurring in the field of nanotechnology, it will be a challenge to keep up with all the possible adverse health effects. As nanoparticles and nanostructures continuously advance and change, their effects on the body may be hard to predict. The property that defines nanoparticles and makes them so useful, their incredibly small size, may also be the most dangerous.

NEGATIVE ENVIRONMENTAL IMPACTS

Nanoparticles have shown potential to clean and protect the environment through adsorption of contaminants. While these nanomaterials are intentionally released to help, there are innumerable nanoparticles in everyday items that are not specifically engineered to interact well with the natural world. Arizona State University researcher Troy Benn asks, "As we inject a nanomaterial into groundwater to remediate a problem are we simultaneously creating a new problem by injecting a material that may have adverse environmental effects?"[29] This problem may become especially evident in water.

Some manufactured nanoparticles have the ability to travel great distances when released into the environment. Nanoparticles have also shown a tendency to form clusters when introduced into groundwater. These clusters can latch onto surface-level contaminants and get carried into groundwater supplies. Once contaminants get into the groundwater they are much more difficult to treat. Flowing groundwater is difficult to access without specialized wells and pumps. The unintentional spread of foreign contaminants may create a serious threat to many **ecosystems**.

Another concern nanoparticles create has to do with their unintended entry into the food chain and drinking water. This entry can ultimately lead nanoparticles into the bodies of organisms that live in these ecosystems. The health risks that waterborne nanoparticles have shown in animals is well documented. In a process called self-aggregation, nanoparticle clusters have the ability to accumulate soil and sediment. This clustering effect can attract biological matter, such as bacteria and other tiny living things. The vast majority of biological structures are larger than these nanoparticles, so even the smallest organism has the potential to take up these particles. This is the start of the upward mobility of nanoparticles in the food chain.

> **WORDS IN CONTEXT**
>
> **ecosystem**
>
> The combination of organisms in a particular area and the environment in which they live.

"There is significant concern in the risk assessment community on the potential for manufactured nanomaterials to transfer and accumulate along a particular food chain," states the National Institute of Standards and Technology (NIST).[30] The food chain starts with microscopic organisms. These are eaten by progressively larger species. This sequence may ultimately reach humans through fish or other animals. Nanoparticles can passively find their way into the body through ingestion of contaminated food and water. These contaminants then have the potential to travel even further if released back into the environment in organisms' waste. All these complex interactions mean that it can be tough to predict where nanoparticles will end up once they are released into the environment.

UNPREDICTABLE NATURE OF NANOPARTICLES

Much of what is known about nanotechnology is limited to laboratory experimentation. In the lab, the behavior of nanoparticles is carefully observed using repeatable and ideal conditions. But outside the lab, the Earth and its diverse environments do not act in this manner. Temperature, pressure, and humidity are all conditions that can be controlled in a laboratory setting but are constantly in flux in the natural world. There is no way to fully predict the forces nature may throw at even a well-understood technology.

To many experts, this is a concerning notion. Unpredictability makes engineers and product manufacturers uneasy about releasing new technology. Very little is known about the chemical stability of many nanoparticles, or how they may evolve once released into the environment. Nanoparticles may lose their intended functionality or undergo structural changes.

Whether these changes make nanoparticles more or less dangerous to humans and the environment is largely unknown. Some argue that the nanotechnology industry is lacking sufficient regulation. "At the moment there is no evidence of any regulation of nanomaterials at all," states **toxicologist** Sam Bruschi.[31] This may be troubling to those who understand the potential health and environmental risks that even the most well-known nanoparticles may pose. While nanotechnology holds incredible promise in many facets of life, scientists and political leaders agree even the most seemingly insignificant change in nanoparticle behavior must not be ignored. There are significant concerns about the unintentional side effects and threats nanotechnology may pose. Even more concerning may be the possibility of intentional harm done with the use of nanomaterials.

WORDS IN CONTEXT

toxicologist
A scientist who studies the effects of drugs, chemicals, and materials on organisms.

NANOTECHNOLOGY AS A WEAPON

In an article analyzing how international laws about weapons should treat nanotechnology, lawyer Robert D. Pinson argues, "A nanotech weapon can be more powerful than any known chemical, biological, or nuclear agent because of the incredibly small size of nanoparticles and their ability to penetrate any material or substance."[32] If nanotechnology is understood and wielded by those who wish to do harm, the results may be devastating. Researchers are working to understand the potential dangers and how to defend against them. Unfortunately, there have not yet been any real-world demonstrations of how to universally protect against nano-based attacks.

A method by which nanotechnology could be used for harm follows the same pathways that beneficial nanotechnology uses. In drug-delivery systems, such as chemotherapy for cancer, nanoparticles are used to more efficiently bring medicine to an affected area. These developments help overcome natural barriers the body puts up against foreign entities. Unfortunately, there is a possibility that nanoshells or other nanoparticles could be engineered to inflict deadly attacks on unsuspecting victims. Instead of delivering helpful substances, these nanoparticles could conceivably be loaded with deadly toxins the human body cannot withstand.

There are worries that nanoparticles could be intentionally released into the environment in high concentrations to inflict damage on purpose. Combining the largely unknown health effects with the increasing popularity of products that use nanomaterials means that the risks could potentially be high. A 2015 study in Paris provided some initial information about exposure to nanoparticles. Researchers found that human-created CNTs were present in the lungs of children in the city. It was unclear how the CNTs found their way into the lungs, and scientists did not know whether they had been intentionally released into the environment. The long-term effects on these individuals are yet to be determined. One fear is that the CNTs could create damage comparable to **asbestos** due to the particle's similar shape.

> **WORDS IN CONTEXT**
>
> **asbestos**
> A material used in building construction known to cause long-term health problems.

Terrorist groups may even combine modern technologies to inflict damage on innocent victims. Flying a drone or unmanned aerial vehicle (UAV) is an easy way to spread chemicals. Easy to purchase and modify, these remote controlled flying machines can be equipped with tanks that can spread chemicals over large areas. This could be a method of quietly dispersing nanoparticles and all of their potentially negative health effects. While the scenario may not be as immediately deadly as explosive attacks or shootings, the thought of it could be enough to have a negative psychological effect. Some of the most frightening consequences of nanotechnology may not be intentional acts of terror. Researchers and engineers may unknowingly be using nanotechnology to propel society towards a technologically created disaster.

TECHNOLOGY GOING TOO FAR

Nanotechnology may play a key role in another important technology called artificial intelligence (AI). While this technology may lead to exciting innovations such as self-driving cars and robotic doctors, many leading technology experts believe AI could be the downfall of human civilization.

"I think we should be very careful about artificial intelligence. . . . Increasingly scientists think there should be some regulatory oversight maybe at the national and international level, just to make sure that we don't do something very foolish," warns Elon Musk, founder of the electric car company Tesla and the rocket company SpaceX.[33] Microsoft cofounder Bill Gates shares this same feeling. He says, "First the machines will do a lot of jobs for us and not be super intelligent. That should be positive if we manage it well. A few decades after that though the intelligence is strong enough to be a concern. I agree with Elon Musk and some others on this and don't understand why some people are not concerned."[34]

Nanowires, CNTs, and nanobattery technology may all play a role in the creation of sophisticated AI. Scientists have begun the work of trying to replicate human brain cells using nanotechnology. The US government has funded development into intelligent computers that

DANGEROUS FABRICS

A material called asbestos was once widely used for its fire-resistant properties. However, scientists eventually realized that breathing in asbestos fibers could cause cancer. This led to a sharp drop in the amount of asbestos used. One downside to CNTs is that they share a similar structure to asbestos. This leads to the possibility of CNTs creating similar health risks.

Unfortunately, it may already be too late to prevent some damage. CNTs have been incorporated into furniture with flame-retardant fabric. The idea was to maintain previous standards for flame resistance while also replacing traditional fabrics that contain hazardous chemicals. There is fear from firefighting organizations that fire teams may be needlessly exposed to cancer-causing agents when extinguishing house fires. Nanotechnology-based fibers may provide fire-resistant benefits without the dangers of the chemicals that are usually used. However, researchers are still working to understand whether there is a risk of these materials coming off the furniture during everyday use and affecting people, animals, and the environment.

can solve complex problems. This has led some researchers to be excited about the possibility and continue to push forward.

Many others, including Musk and Gates, urge caution. The thought of a robot uprising along with the other potential pitfalls of nanotechnology has caused fear to run wild through the minds of many. In some cases, fearful groups and individuals have decided to take action. The fight over the technological future has occasionally turned violent.

SOCIETAL PUSHBACK

On August 8, 2011, a package that was thought to be a prize was received by computer scientist Armando Herrera Corral. It was sent to Mexico City's Monterrey Institute of Technology and Higher Education. His colleague, robotics researcher Alejandro Aceves Lopez, was asked to open the box. Upon opening the box, a small pipe bomb detonated, sending metal fragments into his chest. While Aceves survived the blast, his brother described his condition as serious, stating, "He was in intensive care. He was really bad."[35] This was not the only nanotechnology facility targeted by the threat or act of bombings. The Polytechnic University of Pachuca received a letter bomb, while other Mexican universities with nanotechnology programs had to be evacuated for similar threats.

In 2002, the Mexican government decided to heavily invest in the nanotechnology industry as a way to expand the country's economy. This brought a significant number of researchers and companies into Mexico and other Latin American countries. Multiple groups took exception to this idea. Radical anarchist and environmental groups in Mexico have identified nanotechnology as a threat. They worry it will increase the power of government and technology while simultaneously destroying the environment.

Elon Musk has spoken out about the risks of artificial intelligence. He believes it could be dangerous if its development is not carefully monitored and controlled.

The day after the pipe bomb explosion, a group that calls itself Individuals Tending Towards Savagery (ITS) claimed responsibility. Copies of an anti-nanotechnology rant were found near the explosion and also posted online. The text claimed the targeted organizations would be responsible for catastrophic "nanocontamination." ITS also claimed civilization and technology in general should be held responsible for any future problems. As a part of this manifesto, six other universities and several researchers were also listed as targets of bombings.

ITS believes nanotechnology is the greatest planetary threat. It also mentions other technologies, including genetic engineering, cloning, synthetic biology, geoengineering, and neuroscience as being problematic. Experts fear opinions like this may be spreading, which could lead to increased hostility and more violent attacks in Mexico and around the world.

BRIDGING THE PERCEPTION GAP

While most would agree violence is not the answer, there is still no general consensus on the response to nanotechnology. Barbara Harthorn, the director of the Center of Nanotechnology in Society at the University of California Santa Barbara, states, "There's a huge public that is undecided, which means that opinion is still highly malleable."[36] Educating people about the technology and acknowledging legitimate safety concerns may be the best tools experts have for gaining public support.

THE GRAY GOO PROBLEM

There is a doomsday fear that comes from engineer Eric Drexler's idea of self-assembly. It is called the "gray goo" problem. In this scenario, self-assembling nanostructures would seek out biological matter as a source of construction material and quickly self-replicate. The new structures would continue the same pattern, and the problem would wildly grow out of control until the nanostructures consumed all biological matter on Earth, leaving nothing behind but a gray goo.

Science fiction writers have incorporated this idea into books and movies. The idea has become closely linked to nanotechnology. There is a fear that a rogue scientist could create this scenario. Others believe these all-consuming particles could create themselves and accidently escape a controlled laboratory environment. Either way, the idea is especially scary to a public that knows very little about what happens in nanotechnology facilities.

Drexler has since spoken out against the realism of such an end-of-world scenario. He states, "Runaway replicators, while theoretically possible according to the laws of physics, cannot be built with today's nanotechnology toolset." While this statement offers some assurance against the scenario, it does not deny the possibility. Fortunately, most experts view the risk of a gray goo scenario as being very low.

Quoted in "Nanotechnology Pioneer Slays 'Grey Goo' Myths," *Phys.org*, June 11, 2004. phys.org.

In Harthorn's studies, there was actually much less negative reaction to nanotechnology when compared to genetic engineering. Overall, nanotechnology was not viewed as "messing with nature," unlike perceptions of genetic sciences. However, opinions varied dramatically when breaking down specific uses of nanotechnology. Subjects were quite favorable when asked about nanotechnology being applied for clean energy. When the technology was applied to food or human enhancement, there was a highly negative response.

The Center for Nanotechnology in Society, funded by the National Science Foundation, was created to help scientists, researchers, and the general public understand the opportunities and risks of nanotechnology. It acknowledges the role society plays in the implementation of new technology, stating on its website, "History tells us that new technologies do not enter society on their own. Ultimately, people and societies make technologies and decide how they are used."[37]

REWARDS AND RISKS

There are certainly many effects that may come from the implementation of nanotechnology—both positive ones and negative ones. Nanoparticles have the potential to unlock numerous achievements in health, the environment, and public safety. Unfortunately, nanotechnology also holds the risk of unleashing damaging forces in those same areas. No matter whether the risk is measured in dollars or lives, it is important that these possible threats are recognized and avoided. If not, the consequences may be irreversible. As research and development continue, nanotechnologists are keeping these potential dangers in mind.

Chapter 4

What Is the Future of Nanotechnology?

The future of nanotechnology is bright. While there may be significant risks and hurdles to overcome, that hasn't stopped the research and development of new, groundbreaking applications. Eric Drexler states, "In thinking about nanotechnology today, what's most important is understanding where it leads."[38]

Knowledge about nanotechnology's incredible potential has researchers excited about pushing the limits of fields such as medicine, product materials, electronics, and transportation. Nanotechnology has also inspired a new challenge for the twenty-first century that could transform society's relationship with computing. The number of opportunities for improving society is increasing as the size of technology is decreasing.

HEALING ORGANS WITH A SINGLE TOUCH

A technology developed at Ohio State University's College of Engineering could change the way doctors treat damaged tissues and organs. The new technology is called tissue nanotransfection (TNT). The purpose of TNT is to regenerate cells within the patient's own body, regardless of cell type.

The TNT method uses a nanotechnology-based chip that transports human proteins and the genetic building blocks DNA and RNA. The biological materials are loaded into the chip, housed in arrays of CNTs. The chip is then placed onto the patient's skin where the procedure will take place.

In a process called electroporation, the materials are inserted into skin cells through electrical stimulation. The electrical current pokes holes through the cell membrane, which allows the cell building materials to move from the chip's CNTs into the cells. Once proteins, DNA, and RNA are inside the cells, they begin to convert the adult cells from one type to another. In essence, the procedure reprograms cells that can ultimately replace failing organs.

"With this technology, we can convert skin cells into elements of any organ with just one touch," said the director of the university's Center for Regenerative Medicine & Cell Based Therapies, Dr. Chandan Sen.[39] The procedure is **noninvasive** and simply requires a small electrical zap that is hardly noticed by the patient.

WORDS IN CONTEXT

noninvasive
Not requiring instruments to enter the body.

In studies done on pigs and mice, researchers programmed skin cells to become blood vessel cells. The reprogrammed cells repaired injured legs that had been badly damaged by poor blood flow. Additional tests were performed on mice that had suffered brain injuries from a stroke. After TNT was used to create new nerve-like cells, the mice demonstrated an increase in mental function. Even the research team has been surprised by the results of testing. Dr. Sen believes, "This could be transformative."[40]

The research could lead to extraordinary advances in the medical community. Future uses of TNT in humans may aim to repair or restore injured organs, blood vessels, and nerve cells. Project

Scientists are just beginning to study the potential of nanorobots. In the future, as work continues, these machines may find a wide variety of uses.

researchers do not yet fully understand how all the mechanisms of TNT work, but they believe this nanotechnology-enabled procedure is the beginning of something special.

MOLECULAR ROBOTICS

Many experts have predicted the widespread use of machines known as nanorobots. These tiny devices will be used for a variety of applications. Engineer and entrepreneur Peter Diamandis defines a nanorobot as "a machine that can build and manipulate things precisely at an atomic level."[41] He compares these tiny builders picking up and manipulating atoms such as carbon, nitrogen, hydrogen, and oxygen to the process of building something using LEGO bricks. Many of these nanorobots being developed are inspired by the appearance and function of well-known and understood structures.

One nanorobot being designed combines biological molecules with lab-created synthetic materials. Its body was created from commonly used hard plastic called polystyrene, covered in nanogold and chromium. Using strands of DNA, the body of the robot was attached to catalyst molecules. Once the structure was placed in a solution of hydrogen peroxide, the catalysts induced a reaction that produced bubbles of oxygen. This reaction propels the robot forward. Ultraviolet light can be used to steer it because UV light breaks DNA chains. If the DNA is split, one or more of the nanoengines would drop off, changing the direction of the robot.

Engineers at Ohio State University have proven their capability to create nano-sized mechanical parts that can be used to manipulate DNA. "Nature has produced incredibly complex molecular machines at the nanoscale," stated assistant professor and project leader Carlos Castro.[42] The team is building and using molecules in ways that mimic everyday tools and machines. The future goal of this project is to discover ways that nanorobots can manipulate biological material. Perhaps then, engineers will be able to train and control nanorobots to perform highly complex medical procedures.

If engineers are able to combine the transportation and functional abilities of these nanorobots, there will be a new frontier of sophisticated nanorobotics. One potentially life-saving application of complex nanorobots may involve using them surgically. Such nanorobots could be introduced into the bloodstream and travel to the site of the problem. Once they reach a section of diseased or injured tissue, they may be able to carry out a variety of tasks. They could cut away damaged tissue or even help it regenerate. The nanorobots would be designed to focus only on problematic areas without harming nearby cells. Columbia University researcher Milan Stojanovic explains, "This opens up the possibility of using such molecules to target, treat or kill specific cells without affecting similar healthy cells."[43] The robots would be directed by a tiny onboard computer, which can be remotely controlled by a human surgeon.

In some cases, nanorobots may be better at delicate procedures than human surgeons. One example is found in neurosurgery. The building blocks of the nervous system are cells called neurons. Nano-sized tools have already demonstrated the ability to cut individual neurons without harming surrounding tissue. Being able to work on individual nerve cells could make possible amazingly precise procedures on the brain and spinal cord which were once thought to be impossible or simply too dangerous.

The emergence of surgical nanorobots could also make medical procedures available to more people. The World Health Organization states, "At least 400 million people globally lack access to one or more essential health services."[44] The robots could theoretically be transferred in a single drop of **saline**. This would allow simple transport all over the world, giving less developed countries easy access to cutting-edge medicine.

WORDS IN CONTEXT

saline
A solution of salt and water.

INFECTION-FIGHTING NANOPARTICLES

One of the deadliest infectious diseases in the world is caused by the human immunodeficiency virus (HIV). The virus leads to acquired immunodeficiency syndrome (AIDS), which has no known cure. AIDS weakens the immune system, using the victim's own natural defenses against the body. This allows the virus to reproduce quickly and viciously, and it leaves the body vulnerable to diseases it might normally be able to fight off.

Nanoparticles are being developed to break this cycle. One method for combating HIV is loading bee venom into nanoparticles. Bee venom contains a toxin called melittin. This toxin is capable of damaging the shield that surrounds the virus. Coincidentally, melittin has also been shown to kill tumor cells. This research could lead to potential treatment options for patients diagnosed with cancer. Benny Kottiri, a US government official overseeing the response to HIV/AIDS, spoke about the usefulness of this nano approach: "The potential applications for HIV treatment are incredibly promising."[45]

What makes this technique so promising is its ability to not only attack the virus but also spare the surrounding tissue. The nanoparticles are equipped with a protective bumper, causing them to bounce off the body's much larger normal cells. HIV is much smaller than the nanoparticles. This allows the particles to accurately unleash the bee venom. This technique also shows potential for combatting hepatitis B and C, diseases caused by viruses that affect the liver. Nanotechnology gives researchers hope that they will find cures for diseases that were once thought to be untreatable.

ARTIFICIAL MUSCLE

Much like the inspiration behind nanorobots, scientists and engineers have replicated a natural function using nanomaterials. A breakthrough at the NanoTech Institute at the University of Texas at Dallas created a CNT-based yarn that behaves similarly to natural muscle tissue. "The artificial muscles that we've developed can provide large, ultrafast contractions to lift weights that are 200 times heavier than possible for a natural muscle of the same size," the team behind the yarn announced.[46]

The design is similar to the finger-trap toy. When a finger is placed in each end of the toy, the two fingers become trapped by the helically woven cylinder. In order to be released from the trap, the fingers must be pressed together. This shortens the tube's length while expanding the volume and diameter. Instead of fingers, the CNT yarn is filled with wax and twisted into a coil. When this wax-filled yarn is heated with electricity or a flash of light, the wax expands and causes the yarn length to contract. This muscle-like contraction has led to astonishing results. Each strand of this CNT and wax-based nanoyarn can lift more than 100,000 times its own weight.

ANIMAL INSPIRATION

An unlikely source of nanotechnology inspiration came from the animal kingdom. The gecko has been utilizing nano-sized parts of its body since long before human civilization developed the technology to understand the nano scale. There is a lot to learn from these creatures about how nanotechnology might unfold in the future.

On the gripping side of a gecko's toes, there are approximately one billion hairs which are used as adhesive. The hairs are roughly 200 nanometers wide and long. Their shape gives them their surprising adhesive properties. Geckos are able to run, climb, and stick to nearly any surface without hesitation or risk of falling. For years, scientists were baffled by how the gecko does this. There are no substances or secretions given off by the gecko, but the animal can hold onto a wall like glue. Eventually the nano-sized secret of the tiny hairs was discovered.

One possible use of nano-sized hairs could be in everyday adhesion products. Magnets only work on certain metal surfaces. Nails are good only for wood and other specific materials, and tape products can only support limited weight. If a product modeled after a gecko foot is produced, it could stick to nearly any type of surface. A radical idea of adhesive gloves using this technology is being researched. This could potentially give humans the capability to climb walls or even stick to ceilings in the same manner as the gecko. Much work is still needed to be done for this to happen. Scientists are carefully studying how geckos and other species use natural nanotechnology.

The creators believe this technology will play a key role in future applications. While it is not designed to replace human muscle within the body, one of the team members notes, "These yarn muscles could be used for such diverse applications as robots, catheters for minimally invasive surgery, micromotors . . . and even toys."[47]

SENSING DANGER

Chemical weapons are a frightening reality. These devastating weapons have the ability to kill or injure many people in a single attack. They may prevent victims from breathing, attack the skin, or even shut down the nervous system. Preventing attacks or limiting the number of casualties is a daunting challenge.

One solution is creating a sensor that can detect these deadly chemicals. Nanomaterials are being used to develop this type of technology. The nanoelectromechanical sensor (NEMS) is being tested for this purpose. The NEMS device is an array of silicon **cantilevers**. The 800 nanometer-wide silicon cantilevers behave much like miniature diving boards. When a molecule of a deadly chemical agent hits the sensor, the cantilever is pushed down. This triggers an electrical signal that can be recorded by a computer. Different chemicals can be distinguished by the weight of the molecule that strikes the sensor.

> **WORDS IN CONTEXT**
> **cantilever**
> A beam fixed only at one end.

Sensitivity is a hurdle to overcome in NEMS devices. In initial testing, large quantities of gas were required to effectively trigger and record the experimental attack. This type of simulated attack may be far more severe than what people might experience in a real-world scenario. Even a much smaller amount of gas could cause many injuries or deaths. The challenge will

Graphene plays a role in many potential nanotechnology products. Its great strength could make it useful as a protective layer on a variety of items.

be to make a more sensitive device. If scientists can overcome this hurdle, NEMS devices and other nano-based detection systems may play a critical role in protecting populations against chemical attacks. Layers of protection are important not only for people but also for the various items they use each day.

SURFACE DEFENSES

One of the fastest-growing research areas in nanotechnology is the creation of smart coatings. These coatings are designed to better protect devices from scratches and fractures without the bulky weight of putting them in a hard case. The coatings are also being designed to heal themselves in the event of surface injury.

Ming Yang and colleagues have designed a technology that resembles the structure of human skin. The process involves layering nano-thick layers of materials, including graphene. The research team predicts this smart coating will someday be used to provide a scratch-proof coating on buildings or electronic devices such as smartphones.

In a separate project, engineers were able to make stainless steel surfaces resistant to bacteria. In a process called electrochemical etching, researchers were able to create nano-sized spikes on the surface of the stainless steel. The average protrusion was between 20 and 25 nanometers higher than the steel surface. "It's like a mountain range with both sharp peaks and valleys," says Georgia Tech professor Julie Champion.[48]

These nanospikes were shown to kill the bacteria by puncturing their cell membranes. In testing on mammal cells, there was no evidence of damage. This result was likely due to the size of mammalian cells, which are significantly larger than bacteria. Stainless steel is used to create many products. Equipping these devices with nanospikes may someday make products safer. Future uses of nanospikes in implantable medical devices and food processing equipment may decrease the risk of bacterial infection.

THE GRAND CHALLENGE

In 2015, the White House issued what it called "A Nanotechnology-Inspired Grand Challenge." The ultimate goal of the challenge is to transform the capabilities of computers by bringing together multiple scientific communities. The challenge seeks to accomplish three priorities: "Create a new type of computer that can proactively interpret and learn from data, solve unfamiliar problems using what it has learned, and operate with the energy efficiency of the human brain."[49]

In order to achieve such a monumental task, the challenge has brought together the National Nanotechnology Initiative (NNI), the National Strategic Computing Initiative (NSCI), and the Brain Research through Advancing Innovative Neurotechnologies (BRAIN) program. These three research groups must collaborate and use nanotechnology-inspired devices to tackle the challenge. The ultimate design of the project is to make a computer that is equal to or greater in capability than the human brain.

Nanotechnology-based components of this futuristic, ultraefficient computing device are estimated to take a decade or more to complete. While this vision may be years from completion, nanotechnology is already bringing the future of electronics closer to everyday items. Today's mobile electronic devices are limited by their battery power. A company that specializes in battery technology is close to unlocking exciting potential in electronics and transportation.

ELECTRIC CAR REVOLUTION

Many believe the future of the automobile industry is based on harnessing the power of electricity. While there are electric vehicles (EVs) on the road today, there are limitations based upon current battery technology. An Israeli company called StoreDot looks to implement nanotechnology into the car of the future.

Other companies' strategies are based upon improving the life and mileage a car can receive from a battery. With lithium ion batteries, the current standard, one major limitation is the slow speed of charging. StoreDot is focused on improving this. Its cofounder and CEO, Doron Myersdorf, states, "Fast charging is the critical missing

WORDS IN CONTEXT

ubiquitous
Present, appearing, or found everywhere.

Electric cars will become more and more popular in the coming years. Nanotechnology could improve them by sharply cutting charging time.

link needed to make electric vehicles **ubiquitous**. The currently available battery technology dictates long charging times which makes the EV form of transportation inadequate for the public at large."[50]

The electrical vehicle company Tesla currently uses a charging station called the SuperCharger. The technology takes at least seventy-five minutes to completely charge a drained car battery. StoreDot's technology, the FlashBattery, promises to charge an electric car in five minutes. The FlashBattery uses layers of carbon-based nanomaterials and a proprietary blend of organic compounds to better trap electrons, which allows for an ultrafast charge. The technology could get drivers back on the road faster. It would also allow multiple vehicles to be charged in the time it takes to recharge one today. Overcoming the charging challenges may be enough to entice more drivers to consider purchasing electric vehicles.

Some companies are interested in using StoreDot's technology. One of them is Daimler, the organization that owns the Mercedes-Benz car and truck company. "Electrification of trucks is of top priority at Daimler," states board member Martin Daum.[51] The company views the FlashBattery, which allows nearly 300 miles (480 km) of driving range on a single charge, as a key component of its future. "A large battery that could be recharged in as little as 5 minutes could dramatically change the efficacy of the technology," says car analyst Mike Ramsey.[52]

THE FUTURE IS SMALL

Nanotechnology-inspired advancements are arriving in many areas of science, industry, and daily life. There has been incredible progress since the invention of the AFM. New nanoparticles, nanofibers, and other nanomaterials are developed and improved each year.

Researchers and engineers continue to push products to be stronger, faster, and lighter. Carbon-based nanomaterials have shown benefits in medicine, sports, and the military. Soon there could be products in every facet of life that harness the power of nanotechnology. Society will ultimately determine how far nanotechnology is allowed to go.

Nanotechnology has the potential to be incredibly useful, but it could prove disruptive or even devastating in some cases. Nanoparticles may be able to clean the air, water, and soil, but their own impact on the environment is still being studied. The use of nanotechnology in sporting equipment can boost performance, but this has proven controversial when some athletes are seen as gaining

MOLECULAR ELECTRONICS

As electronic devices become smaller, there must eventually be a trade-off between size and capability. Traditional electronic components will limit how small devices can be. A fresh idea from the nano-world may push these limits further. A group of researchers led by Aurelio Mateo-Alonso at Spain's Basque Excellence Research Center in Polymers are broadening the horizon of nanotechnology-based electronics.

Nanowires are often constructed from carbon, which is shown to conduct electricity well. Electrical circuits are the foundation on which electronic devices are built. An electric circuit is a series of pathways of wires that allows for the flow of electrons. Energy-carrying electrons are supplied by a battery or other power source. The electrons flow through the wires from the power source to the device that requires power.

By implementing nanowires, there is a potential for the production of incredibly small circuits, especially if they can be paired with nano-inspired batteries. The blossoming scientific study of molecular electronics may someday provide society with incredibly small devices. Nanowires and nanocircuits may be a key component to power and control future nanorobots.

an unfair edge. And while doomsday scenarios involving nanoparticles remain science fiction, there are realistic risks to consider as researchers push the boundaries of the field.

The ability to manipulate individual atoms creates a potentially limitless scientific frontier. Each year, breakthroughs in nanotechnology are helping it get closer to the visions for future technology outlined by Richard Feynman in 1959. Much work remains to be done. As Feynman said, "There's plenty of room at the bottom."[53]

Source Notes

Introduction: Saved by Atoms

1. Quoted in "Nanomaterial-Based Bone Regeneration Saves Baby Alpaca," *Nanowerk Nanotechnology*, December 11, 2017. www.nanowerk.com.

2. Quoted in "Nanomaterial-Based Bone Regeneration Saves Baby Alpaca."

3. Quoted in Blaine Friedlander, "Nanotech Transforms Cotton Fibers into Modern Marvel," *Cornell Chronicle*, July 7, 2015. news.cornell.edu.

4. Quoted in "Preparing for Nanotechnology," *Nanotechnology Now*, April 20, 2015. www.nanotech-now.com.

5. Quoted in "About CRN: What Others Say," *Center for Responsible Nanotechnology*, 2008. www.crnano.org.

Chapter 1: How Does Nanotechnology Work?

6. Richard P. Feynman, "There's Plenty of Room at the Bottom," *American Physical Society*, November 18, 2017. www.zyvex.com.

7. Feynman, "There's Plenty of Room at the Bottom."

8. Quoted in JE Hulla, et al. "Nanotechnology: History and Future," *Human and Experimental Toxicology*, 34:12 (2015), pp. 1318–1321.

9. Quoted in Ray Kurzweil, "The Drexler-Smalley Debate on Molecular Assembly," *KurzweilAI*, December 1, 2003. www.kurzweilai.net.

10. "21st Century Nanotechnology Research and Development Act," *GovTrack*, December 4, 2017. www.govtrack.us.

11. Quoted in Zeeya Merali, "This 1,600-Year-Old Goblet Shows That the Romans Were Nanotechnology Pioneers," *Smithsonian Magazine*, September 2013. www.smithsonianmag.com.

12. Quoted in "Richard P. Feynman—Facts," *Nobel Prize*, 2014. www.nobelprize.org.

13. Quoted in Michael Eisenstein, "Self-Assembling DNA Makes Super 3-D Nano Machines," *Wired*, August 6, 2009. www.wired.com.

14. Quoted in Joseph W. Haus. *Fundamentals and Applications of Nanophotonics*. New York: Woodhead Publishing, 2016, p. 341.

Chapter 2: Where Is Nanotechnology Found Today?

15. Quoted in "New Magnet-Based Drug Delivery System Shows Promise for Cancer Treatment," *ScienceDaily*, January 31, 2018. www.sciencedaily.com.

16. Quoted in "Nanotechnology and Oncology: Workshop Summary," *National Academies Press*, 2011. www.nap.edu.

17. "Nanotechnology and Oncology: Workshop Summary."

18. "Nanotechnology and Oncology: Workshop Summary."

19. Quoted in "Is There Such a Thing As a Healthy Tan?" *New York Times*, June 3, 2009. consults.blogs.nytimes.com.

20. Quoted in Kristina Wong, "Full Body Swimsuit Now Banned for Professional Swimmers," *ABC News*, January 4, 2010. abcnews.go.com.

21. Quoted in Devin Taylor, "Nanotechnology in Sports," *UNLV*, 2008. nanotechnology.unlv.edu.

22. Quoted in "Scientists Are Becoming Artists, Thanks to NanoArt," *Public Radio International*, September 30, 2014. www.pri.org.

23. "7 Million Premature Deaths Annually Linked to Air Pollution," *World Health Organization*, March 25, 2014. www.who.int.

24. Quoted in "About CRN: What Others Say."

25. Quoted in Timothy Spence, "Scientists Eye Nanotechnologies to Boost Crop Yields," *Euractiv*, November 23, 2012. www.euractiv.com.

Chapter 3: What Are the Risks of Nanotechnology?

26. Quoted in "About CRN: What Others Say."

27. Quoted in "To Fund Nanotechnology, Shop at Home Depot," *Foresight Institute*, June 1, 2017. www.foresight.org.

28. Quoted in "Health Risks of Nanotechnology: How Nanoparticles Can Cause Lung Damage, and How the Damage Can Be Blocked," *ScienceDaily*, June 11, 2009. www.sciencedaily.com.

29. Quoted in "Nanotechnology Promises Water Resource Gains but Raises Concerns," *WRRC—University of Arizona*, 2010. wrrc.arizona.edu.

30. "Nanoparticles Tracked in a Model Food Chain," *National Nanotechnology Initiative*, n.d. www.nano.gov.

31. Quoted in Anna Salleh, "Nanotech Regulation under the Spotlight," *ABC Science*, July 11, 2008. www.abc.net.au.

32. Robert D. Pinson, "Is Nanotechnology Prohibited by the Biological and Chemical Weapons Conventions," *Berkeley Journal of International Law*, 22:2 (2004), p. 279.

33. Quoted in Peter Holley, "Bill Gates on Dangers of Artificial Intelligence: 'I Don't Understand Why Some People Are Not Concerned,'" *Washington Post*, January 29, 2015. www.washingtonpost.com.

34. Quoted in Peter Holley, "Bill Gates on Dangers of Artificial Intelligence: 'I Don't Understand Why Some People Are Not Concerned.'"

35. Quoted in Leigh Phillips, "Nanotechnology: Armed Resistance," *Nature News*, August 29, 2012. www.nature.com.

36. Quoted in Leigh Phillips, "Nanotechnology: Armed Resistance."

37. "Nanotechnology & Society," *CNS, UCSB, the Regents of the University of California*, 2010. www.cns.ucsb.edu.

Chapter 4: What Is the Future of Nanotechnology?

38. Quoted in "Interview: K. Eric Drexler," *Foresight Update*, 1997. www.islandone.org.

39. Quoted in "Breakthrough Device Heals Organs with a Single Touch," *ScienceDaily*, August 7, 2017. www.sciencedaily.com.

40. Quoted in Simon Makin, "Chip Reprograms Cells to Regenerate Damaged Tissue," *Scientific American*, September 29, 2017. www.scientificamerican.com.

41. Peter Diamandis, "Nanorobots: Where We Are Today and Why Their Future Has Amazing Potential," *Singularity Hub*, May 16, 2016. www.singularityhub.com.

42. Quoted in "How to Create the World's Most Complex 3D-Motion Nanomachines from DNA," *KurzweilAI*, January 12, 2015. www.kurzweilai.net.

43. Quoted in Patrick J. Kiger, "Will Nanobots Perform Surgery in the Future?" *HowStuffWorks*, April 27, 2015. health.howstuffworks.com.

44. "New WHO Data Portal to Help Track Progress towards Universal Health Coverage," *World Health Organization*, December 12, 2016. www.who.int.

45. Quoted in "New Nano Approach Could Cut Dose of Leading HIV Treatment in Half," *ScienceDaily*, February 24, 2017. www.sciencedaily.com.

46. Quoted in "Wax-Filled Nanotech Yarn Behaves Like Super-Strong Muscle," *UT Dallas*, November 15, 2012. www.utdallas.edu.

47. Quoted in Jim Lewis, "Two Types of Artificial Muscle from Nanotechnology," *Foresight Institute*, December 13, 2012. www.foresight.org.

48. Quoted in "Nanotexturing Creates Bacteria-Killing Spikes on Stainless Steel Surfaces," *Georgia Tech*, 2012. www.mc.gatech.edu.

49. Quoted in Lloyd Whitman, "A Nanotechnology-Inspired Grand Challenge for Future Computing," *White House*, October 20, 2015. www.obamawhitehouse.archives.gov.

50. Quoted in Matthew Hughes, "This Israeli Startup Has a Battery That Can Charge an Electric Car in 5 Minutes," *TheNextWeb*, May 11, 2017. thenextweb.com.

51. Quoted in Ryan Browne, "Mercedes Owner Daimler Drives Electric Truck Push with Multi-Million Dollar Investment in StoreDot," *CBNC*, September 18, 2017. www.cnbc.com.

52. Quoted in Ryan Browne, "Mercedes Owner Daimler Drives Electric Truck Push with Multi-Million Dollar Investment in StoreDot."

53. Richard P. Feynman, "There's Plenty of Room at the Bottom."

For Further Research

Books

John Allen, *What Is the Future of Nanotechnology?* San Diego, CA: ReferencePoint, 2017.

Don Nardo, *Nanotechnology and Medicine*. San Diego, CA: ReferencePoint, 2018.

Jeremy J. Ramsden, *Nanotechnology: An Introduction*. Oxford, UK: William Andrew, 2016.

Janet Slingerland, *Nanotechnology*. Minneapolis, MN: Abdo Publishing, 2016.

Bradley Steffens. *Careers in Medical Technology*. San Diego, CA: ReferencePoint, 2017.

Jennifer Swanson, *Super Gear: Nanotechnology and Sports Team Up*. Watertown, MA: Charlesbridge, 2016.

Internet Sources

Rebecca Boyle. "7 Amazing Ways Nanotechnology Is Changing the World," *Popular Science*, November 14, 2012. popsci.com.

John Markoff, "Researchers Build a Working Carbon Nanotube Computer," *New York Times*, September 25, 2013. nytimes.com.

"Nanotechnology News and Updates," *National Institute of Standards and Technology*, n.d. nist.gov.

NPR Staff, "The Future of Nanotechnology and Computers So Small You Can Swallow Them," *NPR*, November 23, 2015. npr.org.

"Optimizing Carbon Nanotube Electrodes," *MIT News*, January 5, 2018. news.mit.edu.

Leigh Phillips, "Nanotechnology: Armed Resistance," *Nature*, August 29, 2012. nature.com.

Websites

National Nanotechnology Coordinated Infrastructure: Careers in Nanotechnology

http://www.nnci.net/careers-nanotechnology

This website is an excellent resource for those who may be considering a career in nanotechnology. This site includes links to educational programs, job postings, and the latest salary statistics.

National Nanotechnology Initiative

https://www.nano.gov

On the National Nanotechnology Initiative (NNI) website, visitors can access information on nanotechnology basics, details on the latest innovations, and links to many legal, ethical, and educational resources.

Nature Nanotechnology

https://www.nature.com/nnano

The website for the publication *Nature* offers readers articles from the latest scientific and technological innovations in nanotechnology.

NBC Learn: Nanotechnology

https://www.nbclearn.com/nanotechnology

This website offers several videos on various topics in nanotechnology. The videos provide visual examples of how science and technology work at the nanometer level.

ScienceDaily: Nanotechnology News

https://www.sciencedaily.com/news/matter_energy/nanotechnology

ScienceDaily is a news website which gives readers access to the latest in global news and research from all sectors of nanotechnology.

Index

Index Continued

Image Credits

Cover: © ktsdesign/Shutterstock Images

4: © Kateryna Kon/Shutterstock Images

5: © Rost9/Shutterstock Images

7: © Monkey Business Images/Shutterstock Images

9: © Magcom/Shutterstock Images

11: © Estate of Francis Bello/Science Source

15: © Dmitry Chulov/Shutterstock Images

18: © dominika zarzycka/Shutterstock Images

23: © ESB Professional/Shutterstock Images

25 (ant): © Irina Kozorog/Shutterstock Images

25 (hair): © Firstsignal/Shutterstock Images

25 (blood cell): © Phonlamai Photo/Shutterstock Images

25 (DNA): © Raj Creationzs/Shutterstock Images

25 (nanotube): © nobeastsofierce/Shutterstock Images

25 (atom): © general-fmv/Shutterstock Images

29: © EPSTOCK/Shutterstock Images

34: © Katsumi Kasahara/AP Images

37: © Ranglen/Shutterstock Images

44: © Magic mine/Shutterstock Images

53: © Kathy Hutchins/Shutterstock Images

58: © Pavel Chagochkin/Shutterstock Images

64: © OliveTree/Shutterstock Images

67: © Seksan 99/Shutterstock Images

About the Author

John Hakala is a freelance writer from Minnesota. Before pursuing a life of writing, he was a nuclear medicine technologist and has published research in the *Journal of Nuclear Medicine Technology*. He currently travels with his wife, Heidi. John is the chief contributor for the blog *Liberty by Choice*.